350

W9-CTN-995

"You were born to live with
magic. We all were, the whole
human race. We're never more
than half alive unless we
have it. . . ."

The Magic May Return

THE MAGIC MAY RETURN

Edited by
Larry Niven

SF
ace books
A Division of Charter Communications Inc.
A GROSSET & DUNLAP COMPANY
51 Madison Avenue
New York, New York 10010

Illustrations by
Alicia Austin

An ACE Book

First Ace printing: Fall 1981
Published Simultaneously in Canada
2 4 6 8 0 9 7 5 3 1
Manufactured in the United States of America

Table of Contents

Introduction

You are about to enter a fantasy world that belongs to Larry Niven.

Two years ago, Ace published THE MAGIC GOES AWAY, a beautifully illustrated book in which Larry Niven told the story of the end of magic. As Sandra Miesel said in her *Afterword* to that book, "Magic no longer exists in our world. But if, as all traditional cultures assert, it ever existed, then why has it disappeared? If magic vanished because its driving energy was depleted, what caused the shortage? And above all, how did people react to the crisis?"

Response to THE MAGIC GOES AWAY was tremendous. Readers loved what Larry Niven did with fantasy, making it as much a game of ideas as the hard science fiction for which he is justly famous. And in that response this book was born.

"I have a proposition for you," said Jim Baen, then Ace's science fiction editor, to Larry Niven. "I will do all of the work and you will take all of the credit." Niven, of course, has been too smart to believe a statement like that for more years than he might like to admit, but the project was a good one, and it prospered. Several well-known science fiction and fantasy authors, admirers of Niven and of THE MAGIC GOES AWAY, wrote their own stories *in the universe that Niven had created*. Larry Niven read each story, and made suggestions from time to time, but each author brought to the work his or her own magic, and each story is a unique achievement in its own right. Then Alicia Austin added *her* magic, with illustrations that make it clear why she has won the Hugo and World Fantasy Award.

Here is the result: THE MAGIC MAY RETURN. Original stories by Poul Anderson and Mildred Downey Broxon, Steven Barnes, Dean Ing, Fred Saberhagen—and the original Larry Niven story about the Warlock, "Not Long Before the End," as a refresher course in the nature of *mana*.

Enjoy.

Not Long Before The End

Larry Niven

A swordsman battled a sorcerer once upon a time.

In that age such battles were frequent. A natural antipathy exists between swordsmen and sorcerers, as between cats and small birds, or between rats and men. Usually the swordsman lost, and humanity's average intelligence rose some trifling fraction. Sometimes the swordsman won, and again the species was improved; for a sorcerer who cannot kill one miserable swordsman is a poor excuse for a sorcerer.

But this battle differed from the others. On one side, the sword itself was enchanted. On the other, the sorcerer knew a great and terrible truth.

We will call him the Warlock, as his name is both forgotten and impossible to pronounce. His parents had known what they were about. He who knows your name has power over you, but he must speak your name to use it.

The Warlock had found his terrible truth in middle age.

By that time he had traveled widely. It was not from choice. It was simply that he was a powerful magician, and he used his power, and he needed friends.

He knew spells to make people love a magician. The Warlock had tried these, but he did not like the side effects. So he commonly used his great power to help those around him, that they might love him without coercion.

He found that when he had been ten to fifteen years in a place, using his magic as whim dictated, his powers would weaken. If he moved away, they returned. Twice he had had to move, and twice he had settled in a new land, learned new customs, made new friends. It happened a third time, and he prepared to move again. But something set him to wondering.

Why should a man's powers be so unfairly drained out of him?

It happened to nations too. Throughout history, those lands which had been richest in magic had been overrun by barbarians carrying swords and clubs. It was a sad truth, and one that did not bear thinking about, but the Warlock's curiosity was strong.

So he wondered, and he stayed to perform certain experiments.

His last experiment involved a simple kinetic sorcery set to spin a metal disc in midair. And when that magic was done, he knew a truth he could never forget.

So he departed. In succeeding decades he moved again and again. Time changed his personality, if not his body, and his magic became more dependable, if less showy. He had discovered a great and terrible truth, and if he kept it secret, it was through compassion. His truth spelled the end of civilization, yet it was of no earthly use to anyone.

So he thought. But some five decades later (the date was on the order of 12,000 B.C.) it occurred to him that all truths find a use somewhere, sometime. And so he built another disc and recited spells over it, so that (like a telephone number already dialed but for one digit) the disc would be ready if ever he needed it.

The name of the sword was Glirendree. It was several hundred years old, and quite famous.

As for the swordsman, his name is no secret. It was Belhap Sattlestone Wirldess ag Miracloat roo Cononson. His friends, who tended to be temporary, called him Hap. He was a barbarian, of course. A civilized man would have had more sense than to touch Glirendree, and better morals than to stab a sleeping woman. Which was how Hap acquired his sword. Or vice versa.

The Warlock recognized it long before he saw it. He was at work in the cavern he had carved beneath a hill, when an alarm went off. The hair rose up, tingling, along the back of his neck. "Visitors," he said.

"I don't hear anything," said Sharla, but there was an uneasiness to her tone. Sharla was a girl of the village who had come to live with the Warlock. That day she had persuaded the Warlock to teach her some of his simpler spells.

"Don't you feel the hair rising on the back of your neck? I set the alarm to do that. Let me just check . . ." He used a sensor like a silver hula hoop set on edge.

"There's trouble coming. Sharla, we've got to get you out of here."

"But . . ." Sharla waved protestingly at the table where they had been working.

"Oh, that. We can quit in the middle. That spell isn't dangerous." It was a charm against lovespells, rather messy to work, but safe and tame and effective. The Warlock pointed at the spear of light glaring through the hoopsensor. "That's dangerous. An enormously powerful focus of mana power is moving up the west side of the hill. You go down the east side."

"Can I help? You've taught me *some* magic."

The magician laughed a little nervously. "Against that? That's Glirendree. Look at the size of the image, the color, the shape. No. You get out of here, and right now. The hill's clear on the eastern slope."

"Come with me."

"I can't. Not with Glirendree loose. Not when it's already got hold of some idiot. There are obligations."

They came out of the cavern together, into the mansion they shared. Sharla, still protesting, donned a robe and started down the hill. The Warlock hastily selected an armload of paraphernalia and went outside.

The intruder was halfway up the hill: a large but apparently human being carrying something long and glittering. He was still a quarter of an hour downslope. The Warlock set up the silver hula hoop and looked through it.

The sword was a flame of mana discharge, an eye-hurting needle of white light. Glirendree, right enough. He knew of other, equally powerful mana foci, but none were portable, and none would show as a sword to the unaided eye.

He should have told Sharla to inform the Brotherhood. She had that much magic. Too late now.

There was no colored borderline to the spear of light.

No green fringe effect meant no protective spells. The swordsman had not tried to guard himself against what he carried. Certainly the intruder was no magician, and he had not the intelligence to get the help of a magician. Did he know *nothing* about Glirendree?

Not that that would help the Warlock. He who carried Glirendree was invulnerable to any power save Glirendree itself. Or so it was said.

"Let's test that," said the Warlock to himself. He dipped into his armload of equipment and came up with something wooden, shaped like an ocarina. He blew the dust off it, raised it in his fist and pointed it down the mountain. But he hesitated.

The loyalty spell was simple and safe, but it did have side effects. It lowered its victim's intelligence.

"Self-defense," the Warlock reminded himself, and blew into the ocarina.

The swordsman did not break stride. Glirendree didn't even glow; it had absorbed the spell that easily.

In minutes the swordsman would be here. The Warlock hurriedly set up a simple prognostics spell. At least he could learn who would win the coming battle.

No picture formed before him. The scenery did not

even waver.

"Well, now," said the Warlock."*Well,* now!"And he reached into his clutter of sorcerous tools and found a metal disc. Another instant's rummaging produced a double-edged knife, profusely inscribed in no known language, and very sharp.

At the top of the Warlock's hill was a spring, and the stream from that spring ran past the Warlock's house. The swordsman stood leaning on his sword, facing the Warlock across that stream. He breathed deeply, for it had been a hard climb.

He was powerfully muscled and profusely scarred. To the Warlock it seemed strange that so young a man should have found time to acquire so many scars. But none of his wounds had impaired motor functions. The Warlock had watched him coming up the hill. The swordsman was in top physical shape.

His eyes were deep blue and brilliant, and half an inch too close together for the Warlock's taste.

"I am Hap," he called across the stream. "Where is she?"

"You mean Sharla, of course. But why is that your concern?"

"I have come to free her from her shameful bondage, old man. Too long have you—"

"Hey, hey, hey. Sharla's my *wife.*"

"Too long have you used her for your vile and lecherous purposes. Too—"

"She stays of her own free will, you nit!"

"You expect me to believe that? As lovely a woman as Sharla, could she love an old and feeble warlock?"

"Do I look feeble?"

The Warlock did not look like an old man. He seemed Hap's age, some twenty years old, and his frame and his musculature were the equal of Hap's. He had not bothered to dress as he left the cavern. In place of Hap's scars, his back bore a tattoo in red and green and gold, an elaborately curlicued penta-gramic design, almost hypnotic in its ex-tradimensional involutions.

"Everyone in the village knows your age," said Hap. "You're two hundred years old, if not more."

"Hap," said the Warlock. "Belhap something-or-other roo Cononson. Now I remember. Sharla told me you tried to bother her last time she went to the village. I should have done something about it then."

"Old man, you lie. Sharla is under a spell. Everybody knows the power of a warlock's loyalty spell."

"I don't use them. I don't like the side effects. Who wants to be surrounded by friendly morons?" The Warlock pointed to Glirendree. "Do you know what you carry?"

Hap nodded ominously.

"Then you ought to know better. Maybe it's not too late. See if you can transfer it to your left hand."

"I tried that. I can't let go of it." Hap cut at the air, restlessly, with his sixty pounds of sword. "I have to sleep with the damned thing clutched in my hand."

"Well, it's too late then."

"It's worth it," Hap said grimly. "For now I can kill you. Too long has an innocent woman been sub-jected to your lecherous—"

"I know, I know." The Warlock changed languages suddenly, speaking high and fast. He spoke thus for

15

almost a minute, then switched back to Rynaldese. "Do you feel any pain?"

"Not a twinge," said Hap. He had not moved. He stood with his remarkable sword at the ready, glowering at the magician across the stream.

"No sudden urge to travel? Attacks of remorse? Change of body temperature?" But Hap was grinning now, not at all nicely. "I thought not. Well, it had to be tried."

There was an instant of blinding light.

When it reached the vicinity of the hill, the meteorite had dwindled to the size of a baseball. It should have finished its journey at the back of Hap's head. Instead, it exploded a millisecond too soon. When the light had died, Hap stood within a ring of craterlets.

The swordsman's unsymmetrical jaw dropped, and then he closed his mouth and started forward. The sword hummed faintly.

The Warlock turned his back.

Hap curled his lip at the Warlock's cowardice. Then he jumped three feet backward from a standing start. A shadow had pulled itself from the Warlock's back.

In a lunar cave with the sun glaring into its mouth, a man's shadow on the wall might have looked that sharp and black. The shadow dropped to the ground and stood up, a humanoid outline that was less a shape than a window view of the ultimate blackness beyond the death of the universe. Then it leapt.

Glirendree seemed to move of its own accord. It hacked the demon once lengthwise and once across, while the demon seemed to batter against an in-

visible shield, trying to reach Hap even as it died.

"Clever," Hap panted. "A pentagram on your back, a demon trapped inside."

"That's clever," said the Warlock, "but it didn't work. Carrying Glirendree works, but it's not clever. I ask you again, do you know what you carry?"

"The most powerful sword ever forged." Hap raised the weapon high. His right arm was more heavily muscled than his left, and inches longer, as if Glirendree had been at work on it. "A sword to make me the equal of any warlock or sorceress, and without the help of demons, either. I had to kill a woman who loved me to get it, but I paid that price gladly. When I have sent you to your just reward, Sharla will come to me—"

"She'll spit in your eye. Now will you listen to me? Glirendree *is* a demon. If you had an ounce of sense, you'd cut your arm off at the elbow."

Hap looked startled. "You mean there's a demon imprisoned in the metal?"

"Get it through your head. *There is no metal.* It's a demon, a bound demon, and it's a parasite. It'll age you to death in a year unless you cut it loose. A warlock of the northlands imprisoned it in its present form, then gave it to one of his bastards, Jeery of Something-or-other. Jeery conquered half this continent before he died on the battlefield, of senile decay. It was given into the charge of the Rainbow Witch a year before I was born, because there never was a woman who had less use for people, especially men."

"That happens to have been untrue."

"Probably Glirendree's doing. Started her glands

up again, did it? She should have guarded against that."

"A year," said Hap. "One year."

But the sword stirred restlessly in his hand. "It will be a glorious year," said Hap, and he came forward.

The Warlock picked up a copper disc. "Four," he said, and the disc spun in midair.

By the time Hap had sloshed through the stream, the disc was a blur of motion. The Warlock moved to keep it between himself and Hap, and Hap dared not touch it, for it would have sheared through anything at all. He crossed around it, but again the Warlock had darted to the other side. In the pause he snatched up something else: a silvery knife, profusely inscribed.

"Whatever that is," said Hap, "it can't hurt me. No magic can affect me while I carry Glirendree."

"True enough," said the Warlock. "The disc will lose its force in a minute anyway. In the meantime, I know a secret that I would like to tell, one I could never tell to a friend."

Hap raised Glirendree above his head and, two-handed, swung it down on the disc. The sword stopped jarringly at the disc's rim.

"It's protecting you," said the Warlock. "If Glirendree hit the rim now, the recoil would knock you clear down to the village. Can't you hear the hum?"

Hap heard the whine as the disc cut the air. The tone was going up and up the scale.

"You're stalling," he said.

"That's true. So? Can it hurt you?"

"No. You were saying you knew a secret." Hap braced himself, sword raised, on one side of the disc, which now glowed red at the edge.

"I've wanted to tell someone for such a long time. A hundred and fifty years. Even Sharla doesn't know." The Warlock still stood ready to run if the swordsman should come after him. "I'd learned a little magic in those days, not much compared to what I know now, but big, showy stuff. Castles floating in the air. Dragons with golden scales. Armies turned to stone, or wiped out by lightning, instead of simple death spells. Stuff like that takes a lot of power, you know?"

"I've heard of such things."

"I did it all the time, for myself, for friends, for whoever happened to be king, or whomever I happened to be in love with. And I found that after I'd been settled for a while, the power would leave me. I'd have to move elsewhere to get it back."

The copper disc glowed bright orange with the heat of its spin. It should have fragmented, or melted, long ago.

"Then there are the dead places, the places where a warlock dares not go. Places where magic doesn't work. They tend to be rural areas, farmlands and sheep ranges, but you can find the old cities, the castles built to float which now lie tilted on their sides, the unnaturally aged bones of dragons, like huge lizards from another age.

"So I started wondering."

Hap stepped back a bit from the heat of the disc. It glowed pure white now, and it was like a sun brought to earth. Through the glare Hap had lost sight of the Warlock.

"So I built a disc like this one and set it spinning.

Just a simple kinetic sorcery, but with a constant acceleration and no limit point. You know what mana is?"

"What's happening to your voice?"

"Mana is the name we give to the power behind magic." The Warlock's voice had gone weak and high.

A horrible suspicion came to Hap. The Warlock had slipped down the hill, leaving his voice behind! Hap trotted around the disc, shading his eyes from its heat.

An old man sat on the other side of the disc. His arthritic fingers, half-crippled with swollen joints, played with a rune-inscribed knife. "What I found out —oh, there you are. Well, it's too late now."

Hap raised his sword, and his sword changed.

It was a massive red demon, horned and hooved, and its teeth were in Hap's right hand. It paused, deliberately, for the few seconds it took Hap to realize what had happened and to try to jerk away. Then it bit down, and the swordsman's hand was off at the wrist.

The demon reached out, slowly enough, but Hap in his surprise was unable to move. He felt the taloned fingers close his windpipe.

He felt the strength leak out of the taloned hand, and he saw surprise and dismay spread across the demon's face.

The disc exploded. All at once and nothing first, it disintegrated into a flat cloud of metallic particles and was gone, flashing away as so much meteorite dust. The light was as lightning striking at one's feet. The sound was its thunder. The smell was vaporized

copper.

The demon faded, as a chameleon fades against its background. Fading, the demon slumped to the ground in slow motion, and faded further, and was gone. When Hap reached out with his foot, he touched only dirt.

Behind Hap was a trench of burnt earth.

The spring had stopped. The rocky bottom of the stream was drying in the sun.

The Warlock's cavern had collapsed. The furnishings of the Warlock's mansion had gone crashing down into that vast pit, but the mansion itself was gone without trace.

Hap clutched his messily severed wrist, and he said, "But what happened?"

"Mana," the Warlock mumbled. He spat out a complete set of blackened teeth. "Mana. What I discovered was that the power behind magic is a natural resource, like the fertility of the soil. When you use it up, it's gone."

"But—"

"Can you see why I kept it a secret? One day all the wide world's mana will be used up. No more mana, no more magic. Do you know that Atlantis is tectonically unstable? Succeeding sorcerer-kings renew the spells each generation to keep the whole continent from sliding into the sea. What happens when the spells don't work any more? They couldn't possibly evacuate the whole continent in time. Kinder not to let them know."

"But . . . that disc."

The Warlock grinned with his empty mouth and ran his hands through snowy hair. All the hair came off in his fingers, leaving his scalp bare and mottled. "Senility is like being drunk. The disc? I told you. A kinetic sorcery with no upper limit. The disc keeps accelerating until all the mana in the locality has been used up."

Hap moved a step forward. Shock had drained half his strength. His foot came down jarringly, as if all the spring were out of his muscles.

"You tried to kill me."

The Warlock nodded. "I figured if the disc didn't explode and kill you while you were trying to go around it, Glirendree would strangle you when the constraint wore off. What are you complaining about? It cost you a hand, but you're free of Glirendree."

Hap took another step, and another. His hand was beginning to hurt, and the pain gave him strength. "Old man," he said thickly. "Two hundred years old. I can break your neck with the hand you left me. And I will."

The Warlock raised the inscribed knife.

"That won't work. No more magic." Hap slapped the Warlock's hand away and took the Warlock by his bony throat.

The Warlock's hand brushed easily aside, and came back, and up. Hap wrapped his arms around his belly and backed away with his eyes and mouth wide open. He sat down hard.

"A knife always works," said the Warlock.

"Oh," said Hap.

"I worked the metal myself, with ordinary blacksmith's tools, so the knife wouldn't crumble when the magic was gone. The runes aren't magic.

They only say—"

"Oh," said Hap. "Oh." He toppled sideways.

The Warlock lowered himself onto his back. He held the knife up and read the markings, in a language only the Brotherhood remembered.

AND THIS, TOO, SHALL PASS AWAY. It was a very old platitude, even then.

He dropped his arm back and lay looking at the sky.

Presently the blue was blotted by a shadow.

"I told you to get out of here," he whispered.

"You should have known better. What's *happened* to you?"

"No more youth spells. I knew I'd have to do it when the prognostics spell showed blank." He drew a ragged breath. "It was worth it. I killed Glirendree."

"Playing hero, at your age! What can I do? How can I help?"

"Get me down the hill before my heart stops. I never told you my true age—"

"I knew. The whole village knows." She pulled him to sitting position, pulled one of his arms around her neck. It felt dead. She shuddered, but she wrapped her own arm around his waist and gathered herself for the effort. "You're so thin! Come on, love. We're going to stand up." She took most of his weight onto her, and they stood up.

"Go slow. I can hear my heart trying to take off."

"How far do we have to go?"

"Just to the foot of the hill, I think. Then the spells will work again, and we can rest." He stumbled. "I'm going blind," he said.

"It's a smooth path, and all downhill."

"That's why I picked this place. I knew I'd have to use the disc someday. You can't throw away knowledge. Always the time comes when you use it, because you have to, because it's there."

"You've changed so. So—so ugly. And you smell." The pulse fluttered in his neck, like a hummingbird's wings. "Maybe you won't want me, after seeing me like this."

"You can change back, can't you?"

"Sure. I can change to anything you like. What color eyes do you want?"

"I'll be like this myself someday," she said. Her voice held cool horror. And it was fading; he was going deaf.

"I'll teach you the proper spells, when you're ready. They're dangerous. Blackly dangerous."

She was silent for a time. Then: "What color were *his* eyes? You know, Belhap Sattlestone whatever."

"Forget it," said the Warlock, with a touch of pique.

And suddenly his sight was back.

But not forever, thought the Warlock as they stumbled through the sudden daylight. When the mana runs out, I'll go like a blown candle flame, and civilization will follow. No more magic, no more magic-based industries. Then the whole world will be barbarian until men learn a new way to coerce nature, and the swordsmen, the damned stupid swordsmen, will win after all.

Earthshade

Fred Saberhagen

When Zalazar saw the lenticular cloud decapitate the mountain, he knew that the old magic in the world was not yet dead. The conviction struck him all in an instant, and with overwhelming force, even as the cloud itself had struck the rock. Dazed by the psychic impact, he turned round shakily on the steep hillside to gaze at the countenance of the youth who was standing beside him. For a long moment then, even as the shockwave of the crash came through the earth beneath their feet and then blasted the air about their ears, Zalazar seemed truly stunned. His old eyes and mind were vacant alike, as if he might never before have seen this young man's face.

"Grandfather." The voice of the youth was hushed, and filled with awe. His gaze went past Zalazar's shoulder, and on up the mountain. "What was that?"

"You saw," said Zalazar shortly. With a hobbling motion on the incline, he turned his attention back to the miracle. "How it came down from the sky. You heard and felt it when it hit. You know as much about it as I do."

Zalazar himself had not particularly noticed one small round cloud, among other clouds of various shape disposed around what was in general an ordinary summer sky. Not until a comparatively rapid relative movement, of something small, unnaturally round, and very white against the high deep blue had happened to catch the corner of his eye. He had looked up directly at the cloud then, and the moment he did that he felt the magic. That distant disk-shape, trailing small patches of ivory fur, had come down in an angled, silent glide that somehow gave the impression of heaviness, of being on the verge of a complete loss of buoyancy and control. The cloud slid, or fell, with a deceptive speed, a speed that became fully apparent to Zalazar only when the long path of its descent at last intersected age-old rock.

"Grandfather, I can feel the magic."

"I'm sure you can. Not that you've ever had the chance to feel anything like it before. But it's something everyone is able to recognize at once." The old man took a step higher on the slope, staring at the mountain fiercely. "You were born to live with magic. We all were, the whole human race. We're never more than half alive unless we have it." He paused for a moment, savoring his own sensations. "Well, I've felt many a great spell in my time. There's no harm in this one, not for us, at least. In fact I think it may possibly bring us some great good."

With that Zalazar paused again, experiencing something new, or maybe something long-forgotten. Was it only that the perceived aura of great spells near at hand brought back memories of his youth? It was more than that, probably. Old wellsprings of divination, caked over by the years, were proving to be still capable of stir and bubble. "All right. Whatever that cloud is, it took the whole top of the mountain with it over into the next valley. I think we should climb up there and take a look." All above was silent now, and apparently tranquil. Except that a large, vague plume of gray dust had become visible above the truncated mountain, where it drifted fitfully in an uncertain wind.

The youth was eager, and they began at once. With his hand upon a strong young arm for support when needed, Zalazar felt confident that his old limbs and heart would serve him through the climb.

They stopped at the foot of an old rock slide to rest, and to drink from a high spring there that the old man knew about. The midsummer grass grew lush around the water source, and with a sudden concern for the mundane Zalazar pointed this out to the boy as a good place to bring the flocks. Then, after they had rested in the shade of a rock for a little longer, the real climb began. It went more easily for Zalazar than he had expected, because he had help at the harder places. They spoke rarely. He was saving his breath, and anyway he did not want to talk or even think much about what they were going to discover. This reluctance was born not of fear, but of an almost childish and still growing anticipation. Whatever else, there was going to be magic in his life again, a vast new store of magic, ebullient and overflowing. And feeding the magic, of course, a small ocean at least of *mana*. Maybe with a supply like that, there would be enough left over to let an old man use some for himself . . . unless it were all used up, maintaining that altered cloud, before they got to it . . .

Zalazar walked and climbed a little faster. *Mana* from somewhere was around him already in the air. Tantalizingly faint, like the first warm wind from the south before the snow has melted, but there indubitably, like spring.

It was obvious to the old man that his companion, even encumbered as he was by bow and quiver on his back and the small lyre at his belt, could have clambered on ahead to get a quick look at the wonders. But the youth stayed patiently at the old man's side. The bright young eyes, though, were for the most part fixed on ahead. Maybe, Zalazar thought, looking at the other speculatively, maybe he's a little more frightened than he wants to admit.

Maybe I am too, he added to himself. But I am certainly going on up there, nevertheless.

At about midday they reached what was now the mountaintop. It was a bright new tableland, about half a kilometer across, and as flat now as a certain parade ground that the old man could remember. The sight also made Zalazar think imaginatively of the stump of some giant's neck or limb; it was rimmed with soil and growth resembling scurfy skin, it was boned and veined with white rocks and red toward the middle, and it bubbled here and there with pure new springs, the blood of Earth.

From a little distance the raw new surface looked preternaturally smooth. But when you were really near, close enough to bend down and touch the faint new warmth of it, you could see that the surface left by the mighty plane was not *that* smooth; no more level, perhaps, than it might have been made by a small army of men with hand tools, provided they had been well supervised and induced to try.

The foot trail had brought them up the west side of what was left of the mountain. The strange cloud in its long, killing glide had come down also from the west, and had carried the whole mass of the mountaintop off with it to the east. Not far, though. For now, from his newly gained advantage upon the western rim of the new tabletop, Zalazar could see

AUSTIN - 1981

the cloud again.

It was no more than a kilometer or so away. Looking like some giant, snow white, not-quite-rigid dish. It was tilted almost on edge, and it was half sunken into the valley on the mountain's far side, so that the place where Zalazar stood was just about on a horizontal level with the enormous dish's center.

"Come," he said to his young companion, and immediately led the way forward across the smoothed-off rock. The cloud ahead of them was stirring continually, like a sail in a faint breeze, and Zalazar realized that the bulk of it must be still partially airborne. Probably the lower curve of its circular rim was resting or dragging on the floor of the valley below, like the basket of a balloon ready to take off. In his youth, Zalazar had seen balloons, as well as magic and parade grounds. In his youth he had seen much.

As he walked, the raw *mana* rose all around him from the newly opened earth. It was a maddeningly subtle emanation, like ancient perfume, like warm air from an oven used yesterday to bake the finest bread. Zalazar inhaled it like a starving man, with mind and memory as well as lungs. It wasn't enough, he told himself, to really do anything with. But it was quite enough to make him remember what the world had once been like, and what his own role in the world had been.

At another time, under different conditions, such a fragrance of *mana* might have been enough to make the old man weep. But not now, with the wonder of the cloud visible just ahead. It seemed to be waiting for him. Zalazar felt no inclination to dawdle, sniffing the air nostalgically.

There was movement on the planed ground just before his feet. Looking down without breaking stride, Zalazar beheld small creatures that had once been living, then petrified into the mountain's fabric by the slow failure of the world's *mana,* now stirring with gropings.back toward life. Under his sandaled foot he felt the purl of a new spring, almost alive. The sensation was gone in an instant, but it jarred him into noticing how quick his own strides had suddenly become, as if he too were already on the way to rejuvenation.

When they reached the eastern edge of the tabletop, Zalazar found he could look almost straight down to where a newly created slope of talus began far below. From the fringes of this great mass of rubble that had been a mountaintop, giant trees, freshly slain or crippled by the landslide, jutted out here and there at deathly angles. The dust of the enormous crash was still persisting faintly in the breeze, and Zalazar thought he could still hear the last withdrawing echoes of its roar . . .

"Grandfather, look!"

Zalazar raised his head quickly, to see the tilted lens-shape of the gigantic cloud bestirring itself with new apparent purpose. Half rolling on its circular rim, which dragged new scars into the valley's grassy skin below, and half lurching sideways, it was slowly, ponderously making its way back toward the mountain and the two who watched it.

The cloud also appeared to be shrinking slightly. Mass in the form of vapor was fuming and boiling away from the vast gentle convexities of its sides. There were also sidewise gouts of rain or spray, that woke in Zalazar the memory of ocean waterspouts. Thunder grumbled. Or was it only the cloud's weight, scraping at the ground? The extremity of the round, mountain-chopping rim looked hard and deadly as a scimitar. Then from the rim inwards the appearance of the enchanted cloudstuff altered gradually, until at the hub of the great wheel a dullard might have thought it only natural.

Another wheelturn of a few degrees. Another thunderous lurch. And suddenly the cloud was a hundred meters closer than before. Someone or something was maneuvering it.

"Grandfather?"

Zalazar spoke in answer to the anxious tone. "It won't do us a bit of good to try to run away." His own voice was cheerful, not fatalistic. The good feeling that he had about the cloud had grown stronger, if anything, the nearer he got to it. Maybe his prescient sense, long dormant, had been awakened into something like acuity by the faint accession of *mana* from the newly opened earth. He could tell that the *mana* in the cloud itself was vastly stronger. "We don't have to be afraid, lad. They don't mean us any harm."

"They?"

"There's—someone—inside that cloud. If you can still call it a cloud, as much as it's been changed."

"*Inside* it? Who could that be?"

Zalazar gestured his ignorance. He felt sure of the fact of the cloud's being inhabited, without being able to say how he knew, or even beginning to understand how such a thing could be. Wizards had been known to ride *on* clouds, of course, with a minimum of alteration in the material. But to alter one to this extent . . .

The cloud meanwhile continued to work its way closer. Turn, slide, ponderous hop, gigantic bump and scrape. It was now only about a hundred meters beyond the edge of the cliff. And now it appeared that something new was going to happen.

The tilted, slowly oscillating wall that was the cloudside closest to the cliff had developed a rolling boil quite near its center. Zalazar judged that this hub of white disturbance was only slightly bigger than a man. After a few moments of development, during which time the whole cloud-mass slid majestically still closer to the cliff, the hub blew out in a hard but silent puff of vapor. Where it had been was now an opening, an arched doorway into the pale interior of the cloud.

A figure in human shape, that of a woman nobly dressed, appeared an instant later in this doorway. Zalazar, in the first moment that he looked directly at her, was struck with awe. In that moment all the day's earlier marvels shrank down, for him, to dimensions hardly greater than the ordinary; they had been but fitting prologue. This was the great true wonder.

He went down at once upon one knee, averting his gaze from the personage before him. And without raising his eyes he put out a hand, and tugged fiercely at his grandson's sleeve until the boy had knelt down too.

Then the woman who was standing in the doorway called to them. Her voice was very clear, and it seemed to the old man that he had been waiting all his years to hear that call. Still the words in themselves were certainly prosaic enough. "You men!" she cried. "I ask your help."

Probably *ask* was not the most accurate word she could have chosen. Zalazar heard himself babbling some reply immediately, some extravagant promise whose exact wording he could not recall a moment later. Not that it mattered, probably. Commitment had been demanded and given.

His pledge once made, he found that he could raise his eyes again. Still the huge cloud was easing closer to the cliff, in little bumps and starts. Its lower flange was continually bending and flowing, making slow thunder against the talus far below, a roaring rearrangement of the fallen rock.

"I am Je," the dazzlingly beautiful woman called them in an imperious voice. Her robes were rich blue, brown, and an ermine that made the cloud itself look gray. "It is written that you two are the men I need to find. Who are you?"

The terrible beauty of her face was no more than a score of meters distant now. Again Zalazar had to look away from its full glory. "I am Zalazar, mighty Je," he answered, in a breaking voice. "I am only a poor man. And this is my innocent grandson— Bormanus." For a moment he had had to search to find the name. "Take pity on us!"

"I mean to take pity on the world, instead, and use you as may be necessary for the world's good," the goddess answered. "But what worthier fate can mortals hope for? Look at me, both of you."

Zalazar raised his eyes again. The woman's countenance was once more bearable. Even as he looked, she turned her head as if to speak or otherwise com-

municate with someone else behind her in the cloud. Zalazar could see in there part of a corridor, and also a portion of some kind of room, all limned in brightness. The white interior walls and overhead were all shifting slightly and continually in their outlines, in a way that suggested unaltered cloudstuff. But the changes were never more than slight, the largescale shapes remaining as stable as those of a wooden house. And the lady stood always upright upon a perfectly level deck, despite the vast oscillations of the cloud, and its turning as it shifted ever closer to the cliff.

Her piercing gaze returned to Zalazar. "You are an old man, mortal, at first glance not good for much. But I see that there is hidden value in you. You may stand up."

He got slowly to his feet. "My lady Je, it is true that once my hands knew power. But the long death of the world has crippled me."

The goddess' anger flared at him like a flame. "Speak not to me of death! I am no mere mortal subject to Thanatos." Her figure, as terrible as that of any warrior, as female as any succubus of love, was now no more than five meters from Zalazar's half-closed eyes. Her voice rang as clearly and commandingly as before. Yet, mixed with its power was a tone of doomed helplessness, and this tone frightened Zalazar on a deeper level even than did her implied threat.

"Lady," he murmured, "I can but try. Whatever help you need, I will attempt to give it."

"Certainly you will. And willingly. If in the old times your hands knew power, as you say, then you will try hard and risk much to bring the old times back again. You will be glad to hazard what little of good your life may have left in it now. Is it not so?"

Zalazar could only sign agreement, wordlessly.

"And the lad with you, your grandson. Is he your apprentice too? Have you given him any training?"

"In tending flocks, no more. In magic?" The old man gestured helplessness with gnarled hands. "In magic, great lady Je? How could I have? Everywhere that we have lived, the world is dead. Or so close to utter deadness that—"

"I have said that you must not speak to me of death! I will not warn you again. Now, it is written that . . . both of you must come aboard. Yes, both, there will be use for both." And, as if the goddess were piloting and powering the cloud with her will alone, the whole mass of it now tilted gently, bringing her spotless doorway within easy stepping distance of the lip of rock.

*   *   *   *

Now Zalazar and Bormanus with him were surrounded by whiteness, sealed into it as if by mounds of glowing cotton. White cushioned firmness served their feet as floor or deck, as level always for them as for their divine guide who walked ahead. Whiteness opened itself ahead of her, and sealed itself again when Bormanus had passed, walking close on Zalazar's heels.

The grinding of tormented rock and earth below could no longer be heard as the Lady Je, her robes of ermine and ultramarine and brown swirling with her long strides, led them through the cloud. Almost there was no sound at all. Maybe a little wind,

Zalazar decided, very faint and sounding far away. He had the feeling that the cloud, its power and purpose somehow regained, had risen quickly from the scarred valley and was once more swiftly airborne.

Je came to a sudden halt in the soft pearly silence, and stretched forth her arms. Around her an open space, a room, swiftly began to define itself. In moments there had grown an intricately formed chamber, as high as a large temple, in which she stood like a statue with her two puny mortal figures in attendance.

Then Zalazar saw that there was one other in the room with them. He muttered something, and heard Bormanus at his side give a quick intake of breath.

The bier or altar at the room's far end supported a figure that might almost have been a gray statue of a tormented man, done on a heroic scale. The figure was youthful, powerful, naked. With limbs contorted it lay twisted on one side. The head was turned in a god's agony so that the short beard jutted vertically.

But it was not a statue. And Zalazar could tell, within a moment of first seeing it, that the sleep that held it was not quite—or not yet—the sleep of death. He had been forbidden to mention death to Je again, and he would not do so.

With a double gesture she beckoned both mortals to cross the room with her to stand beside the figure. While Zalazar was wondering what he ought to say or do, his own right hand moved out, without his willing it, as if to touch the statue-man. Je, he saw, observed this, but she said nothing; and with a great effort of his will Zalazar forced his own arm back to his side. Meanwhile Bormanus at his side was standing still, staring, as if unable to move or speak at all.

Je spoke now as if angry and disappointed. "So, what buried value have you, old man? If you can be of no help in freeing my ally, then why has it been ordained for you to be here?"

"Lady, how should I know?" Zalazar burst out. "I am sorry to disappoint you. I knew something, once, of magic. But . . ." As for even understanding the forces that could bind a god like this, let alone trying to undo them . . . Zalazar could only gesture helplessly. At last he found words. "Great lady Je, I do not even know who this is."

"Call him Phaeton."

"Ah, great gods," Zalazar muttered, shocked and near despair.

"Yes, mortal, indeed we are. As well you knew when you first saw us."

"Yes, I knew . . . indeed." In fact he had thought that all the gods were long dead, or departed from the world of humankind. "And why is he—like this?"

"He has fallen in battle, mortal. I and he and others have laid siege to Cloudholm, and it has been a long and bitter fight. We seek to free his father, Helios, who lies trapped in the same kind of enchantment there. Through Helios' entrapment, the world of old is dying. Have you heard of Cloudholm, old mortal? Among men it is not often named."

"Ah. I have heard something. Long ago . . ."

"It stifles the *mana*-rain that Helios cast ever on the Earth. With a fleet of cloudships like this one, we hurled ourselves upon its battlements—and were defeated. Most of the old gods lie now in tormented slumber, far above. A few have switched sides willingly. And all our ships save this one were destroyed."

"How could they dare?" The words burst from Bormanus, the first he had uttered since boarding the cloud-vessel. Then he stuttered, as Je's eyes burned at him: "I mean, who would dare try to destroy such ships? And who would have the power to do it?"

The goddess looked at the boy a moment longer, then reached out and took him by the hand. "Lend me your mortal fingers here. Let us see if they will serve to drain enchantment off." Bormanus appeared to be trying to draw back, but his hand, like a baby's, was brought out forcibly to touch the statue-figure's arm. And Zalazar's hand went out on its own once more; this time he could not keep it back, or perhaps he did not dare to try. His fingers spread on rounded arm-muscle, thicker by far than his own thigh. The touch of the figure made him think more of frozen snake than flesh of god. And now, Zalazar felt faint with sudden terror. Something, some great power, was urging the freezing near-death to desert its present captive and be content with Zalazar and Bormanus instead. But that mighty urging was mightily opposed, and came to nothing. At last, far above Zalazar's head, as if between proud kings disputing across some infant's cradle, a truce was reached. For the moment. He was able to withdraw his hand unharmed, and watched as Bormanus did the same.

The goddess Je sighed. It was a world-weary sound, close to defeat yet still infinitely stubborn. "And yet I am sure that there is *something* in you, old man . . . or possibly in your young companion here.

Something that in the end will be of very great importance. Something that must be found . . . though I see, now, that you yourselves can hardly be expected to be aware of what it is."

He clasped his hands. "Oh great lady Je, we are only poor humans . . . mortals . . ."

"Never mind. In time I will discover the key. What is written anywhere, I can eventually read."

Zalazar was aware now of a strong motion underneath his feet. Even to weak human senses it was evident that the whole cloud was now in purposeful and very rapid flight.

"Where are we going?" Bormanus muttered, as if he were asking the air itself. He was a very handsome youth, with dark and curly hair.

"We return to the attack, young mortal. If most of our fleet has been destroyed, well, so too are the defenses of Cloudholm nearly worn away. One more assault can bring it into my hands, and set its prisoners free."

Zalazar had been about to ask some question, but now a distracting realization made him forget what it was. He had suddenly become aware that there was some guardian presence, sprite or demon he thought, melded with the cloud, driving and controlling it on Je's commands. It drew for energy on some vast internal store of *mana*, a treasure trove that Zalazar could only dimly sense.

Now, in obedience to Je's unspoken orders, the light inside the room or temple where they stood was taking on a reddish tinge. And now the cloud-carvings were disappearing from what Zalazar took to be the forward wall. As Je faced in that direction, pictures began to appear there magically. These were of a cloudscape first, then of an earthly plain seen from a height greater than any mountain's. Both were passing at fantastic speed.

Je nodded as if satisfied. "Come," she said, "and we will try your usefulness in a new way." With a quick gesture she opened the whiteness to one side, and overhead. A stair took form even as she began to climb it. "We will see if your value lies in reconnoitering the enemy."

Clinging to Bormanus' shoulder for support, Zalazar found that the stairs were not as hard to negotiate as he had feared, even when they shifted form from one step to the next. Then there was a sudden gaping purple openness above their heads. "Fear not," said Je. "My protection is upon you both, to let you breathe and live."

Zalazar and Bormanus mounted higher. Wind shrieked thinly now, not in their faces but round them at some little distance, as if warded by some invisible shield. Then abruptly the climbing stair had no more steps. Zalazar thought that they stood on an open deck of cloud, under a bright sun in a dark sky, in some strange realm of neither day nor night. The prow of the cloudship that he rode upon was just before him; he stood as if on the bridge of some proud ocean vessel, looking out over deck and rounded bow, and a wild vastness of the elements beyond.

Not that the ship was borne by anything as small and simple as an earthly sea. The whole globe of Earth was already so far below that Zalazar could now begin to see its roundness, and still the

cloudship climbed. All natural clouds were far below, clinging near the great curve of Earth, though rising here and there in strong relief. At first Zalazar thought that the star-pierced blackness through which they flew was empty of everything but passing light. But presently—with, as he sensed, Je's unspoken aid—he began to be able to perceive structure in the thinness of space about him.

"What do you see now, my sage old man? And you, my clever youth?" Je's voice pleaded even as it mocked and commanded. Her fear and puzzlement frightened Zalazar again. For the first time now he knew true regret that he had followed his first impulse and climbed a chopped-off mountain. Where now was the good result that prescience had seemed to promise?

"I see only the night ahead of us," responded Bormanus. His voice sounded remote, as if he were half asleep.

"I . . . see," said Zalazar, and paused with that. Much was coming clear to him, but it was going to be hard to describe. The cloud structures far below, so heavy with their contained water and their own mundane laws, blended almost imperceptibly into the base of something much vaster, finer, and more subtle. Something that filled the space around the Earth, from the level of those low clouds up to the vastly greater altitude at which Zalazar now stood. And higher still . . . his eyes, as if ensnared now by those faery lines and arches, followed them upward and outward and ever higher still. The lines girdled the whole round Earth, and rose . . .

And rose . . .

Zalazar clutched out for support. Obligingly, a stanchion of cloudstuff grew up and hardened into place to meet his grasp. He did not even look at it. His eyes were fixed up and ahead, looking at Cloudholm.

Imagine the greatest castle of legend. And then go beyond that, and beyond, till imagination knows itself inadequate. Two aspects dominate: first, an almost invisible delicacy, with the appearance of a fragility to match. Secondly, almost omnipotent power—or, again, its seeming. Size was certainly a component of that power. Zalazar had never tried to, or been able to, imagine anything as high as this. So high that it grew near only slowly, though the cloudship was racing toward it at a speed that Zalazar would have described as almost as fast as thought.

Then Zalazar saw how, beyond Cloudholm, a thin crescent of Moon rose wonderfully higher still; and again, beyond that, burned the blaze of Sun, a jewel in black. These sights threw him into a sudden terror of the depths of space. No longer did he marvel so greatly that Je and her allied powers could have been defeated.

"Great lady," he asked humbly, "what realm, whose dominion is this?"

"What I need from you, mortal, are answers, not questions of a kind that I can pose myself." Je's broad white hand swung out gently to touch him on the eyes. Her touch felt surprisingly warm. Her voice commanded: "Say what you see."

The touch at once allowed him to see more clearly. But he stuttered, groping for words. What he was suddenly able to perceive was that the Sun lived at the core of a magnificent, perpetual explosion, the expanding waves of which were as faint as Cloudholm itself, but none the less glorious for that. These waves moved in some medium far finer than the air, more tenuous than even the thinning air that had almost ceased to whistle with the cloudship's passage. And the waves of the continual slow sun-explosion bore with them a myriad of almost infinitesimal particles, particles that were heavy with *mana*, though they were almost too small to be called solid.

And there were the lines, as of pure force, in space. In obedience to some elegant system of laws they bore the gossamer outer robes of the Sun itself, to wrap the Earth with delicate energy . . . and the *mana* that flowed outward from the Sun, great Zeus but there was such a flood of it!

The Earth was bathed in warmth and energy—but not in *mana*, Zalazar suddenly perceived. That flow had been cut off by Cloudholm and its spreading wings. (Yes, Zalazar could see the pinions of enchantment now, raptor-wings extending curved on two sides from the castle itself, as if to embrace the whole Earth—or smother it.) Through them the common sunlight flowed on unimpeded, to make the surface of the world flash blue and ermine white. But all the inner energies of magic were cut off . . .

Zalazar realized with a start that he was, or just had been, entranced and muttering, that someone with a mighty grip had just shaken his arm, that a voice of divine power was urging him to speak up, to make sense in what he reported of his vision.

"Tell clearly what you see, old man. The wings,

you say, spread out from Cloudholm to enfold the Earth. That much I knew already. Now say what their weakness is. How are they to be torn aside?"

"I . . . I . . . the wings are very strong. They draw sustaining power from the very flow of *mana* that they deny the Earth. Some of the particles that hail on them go through—but those are without *mana*. Many of the particles and waves remain, are trapped by the great wings and drained of *mana* and of other energies. Then eventually they are let go."

"Old fool, what use are you? You tell me nothing I do not already know. Say, where is the weakness of the wings? How can our Earth be fed?"

"Just at the poles . . . there is a weakness, sometimes, a drooping of the wings, and there a little more *mana* than elsewhere can reach the Earth."

Suddenly faint, Zalazar felt himself begin to topple. He was grabbed, and upheld, and shaken again. "Tell more, mortal. What power has created Cloudholm?"

"What do I know? How can I see? What can I say?"

He was shaken more violently than before, until in his desperate fear of Je he cried: "Great Apollo himself could not learn more!"

He was released abruptly, and there was a precipitous silence, as if even Je had been shocked by Zalazar's free use of that name, the presence of whose owner only his mother Leto and his father Zeus could readily endure. Then Zalazar's eyes were brushed again by Je's warm hand, and he came fully to himself.

Cloudholm was bearing down on them. "And

Helios is trapped up there?" Zalazar wondered aloud. "But why, and how?"

"Why?" The bitterness and soft rage in Je's voice were worthy of a goddess. "Why, I myself helped first to bind him. Was I made to do that, after opposing him and bringing on a bitter quarrel? I do not know. Are even we deities the playthings of some overriding fate? What was Helios' sin, for such a punishment? And what was mine?"

Again Zalazar had to avert his gaze, for Je's beauty glowed even more terribly than before. And at the same time he had to strive to master himself, hold firm his will against the hubris that rose up in him and urged him to reach for the role of god himself. Such an opportunity existed, would exist, fore-knowledge told him, and it was somewhere near at hand. If he only . . .

His internal struggle was interrupted by the re-alization that the cloudship no longer moved. Look-ing carefully, Zalazar could see that it had come to rest upon an almost insubstantial plain.

Straight ahead of him now, the bases of the walls of Cloudholm rose. And there was a towering gate.

Je was addressing him almost calmly again. "If your latent power, old mortal, is neither of healing nor of seeing, then perhaps it lies in the realm of war. That is the way we now must pass. Kneel down."

Zalazar knelt. The right hand of the goddess closed on his and drew him to his feet again. He arose on lithely muscular legs, and saw that the old clothing in which he had walked the high pasturelands had been transformed. He was clad now in silver cloth, a fabric worked with a fine brocade. His garments hung on him as solidly as chain mail yet felt as soft and light as silk. They were at once the clothing and the armor of a god. In Zalazar's right hand, grown young and muscular, a short sword had appeared. The weapon was of some metal vastly different from that of his garments, and yet he could feel that its power was at least their equal. On his left arm now hung a shield of dazzling brightness, but seemingly of no more than a bracelet's weight.

The front of the cloudship divided and opened a way for the man who had been the old herdsman Zalazar. The thin cloudstuff of the magic plain swirled and rippled round his boots of silver-gray. His feet were firmly planted, and though he could plainly see the sunlit Earth below, he knew no fear that he might fall.

He glanced behind him once, and saw the cloudship altering, disintegrating, and knew that the nameless demon who had sustained it had come out now at Je's command, to serve her in some other way.

Then Zalazar faced ahead. He could see, now, how much damage the great walls of Cloudholm had sustained, and what had caused the damage. Other cloudships, their insubstantial wreckage mixed with that of the walls they had assailed, lay scattered across the plain and piled at the feet of those enduring, fragile-looking towers. Nor were the wrecked ships empty. With vision somehow granted him by Je, Zalazar could see that each of them held at least one sleep-bound figure of the stature of a god or demi-god. They were male or female, old-looking or young, of divers attributes. All were caught and held,

like Phaethon, by some powerful magic that imposed a quiet if not always a peaceful slumber.

Now, where was Je herself? Zalazar realized suddenly that he could see neither the goddess nor her attendant demon. He called her name aloud.

Do not seek me, her voice replied, whispering just at his ear. *Make your way across the plain, and force the castle gates. With my help you can do it, and I shall be with you when my help is needed.*

Zalazar shrugged his shoulders. With part of his mind he knew that his present feelings of power and confidence were unnatural, given him by the goddess for her own purposes. But at the same time he could not deny those feelings—nor did he really want to. Feeling enormously capable, driven by an urge to prove what this divine weapon in his new right hand could do, he shrugged his shoulders again, loosening tight new muscles for action. Beside him, Bormanus, who had not been changed, was looking about in all directions alertly. With one hand the lad gripped tightly the small lyre at his belt, but he gave no other sign of fear. Then suddenly he raised his other hand and pointed.

Coming from the gates of Cloudholm, which now stood open, already halfway across the wide plain between, a challenger was treading thin white cloud in great white boots.

Zalazar, watching, raised his sword a little. Still the goddess was letting him know no fear. He who approached was a red-bearded man, wearing what looked like a winged Nordik helm, and other equipment to match. He was of no remarkable height for a hero, but as he drew near Zalazar saw that his arms and shoulders under a tight battle-harness were of enormous thickness. He balanced a monstrous war-hammer like a feather in one hand.

I should know who this is, Zalazar thought. But then the thought was gone, as quickly as it had come. Je manages her tools too well, he thought again, and then that idea too was swept from his mind.

The one approaching came to a halt, no more than three quick strides away. "Return to Earth, old Zalazar," he called out, jovially enough. "My bones already ache with a full age of combat. I yearn to let little brother Hypnos whisper in my ear, so I can lie down and rest. I don't know why Je bothered to bring you here; the proper time for humans to visit Cloudholm is long gone, and again, is not yet come."

"Save your riddles," Zalazar advised him fearlessly. This, he thought, in a moment of great glory and pride, this is what it is like to be a god. And in his heart he thanked Je for this moment, and cared not what might happen in the next.

"Oho," Red-beard remarked good-humoredly. "Well then, it seems we must." And the sword and hammer leapt together of themselves, with a blare as of all war-trumpets in the world, and a clash as of all arms. It lasted endlessly, and at the same time it seemed to take no time at all. Zalazar thought that he saw Red-beard fall, but when he bent with some intention of dealing a finishing stroke, the figure of his opponent had vanished. Save for Bormanus, who had prudently stepped back from the clash, he was apparently alone.

Well fought! Je's voice, from invisible lips, whispered beside his ear. There was new excitement in

the words, an undertone of savage triumph.

Zalazar, triumphant too—and at the same time knowing an undercurrent of dissatisfaction, for these deeds were not his of his own right—moved on toward the open gate. He had gone a dozen strides when something—he thought not Je—urged him to look back. When he did, he could now see Red-beard, hammer still in hand, stretched out upon the cloud. There was no sign of blood or injury. At Red-beard's ear a winged head was hovering, whispering a compulsion from divine lips. And on the face of the fallen warrior there was peace.

Why do you pause? Je demanded in her hidden voice. She required no answer, but Zalazar must go on. All Je's attention, and Zalazar's too, was bent now upon the open castle gate. It slammed shut of itself when he was still a hundred strides away. Now he could see that what he had taken for carved dragon heads on either side of the portal were alive, turning fanged jaws toward him.

Zalazar glanced at the lad who was walking so trustingly at his side, and for the first time since landing on the cloud-plain he knew anxiety. "Lady Je," he prayed in a whisper, "I crave your protection for my grandson as well as for myself."

I give what protection I can, to those I need. And I foresee now that I will need him, later on . . .

The dragons guarding the gate stretched out their necks when Zalazar came near; fangs like bunched knives drove at him. The shield raised upon his left arm took the blows. The sword flashed left, lashed right.

Zalazar stepped back, gasping; he looked to see

that Bormanus, who had kept clear, was safe. Then Zalazar willed the swordblade at the great cruciform timbers of the gate itself. They splintered, shuddered, and swung back.

Je's triumph was a shrill scream, almost soundless, inarticulate.

Zalazar knew that he must still go forward, now into Cloudholm itself. He balanced the shield upon his left arm, hefted the sword again in his right hand. He drew a deep breath, of ample-seeming air, and entered the palace proper.

He came to door after door, each taller and more magnificent than the last, and each swung open of itself to let him in. Around him on every hand there towered shapes that should have been terrible, though he could see them only indistinctly. Something told him which way he must go. And he pressed on, through one royal hall and chamber after another . . .

. . . until he had entered that which he knew must be the greatest hall of all. At the far end of it, very distant from where he stood, Zalazar saw the Throne of the World. It was guarded by a wall of flame, and it was standing vacant.

As Zalazar's feet brought him closer to the fire, he saw that it was centered on a plinth of cloud, that supported another man-like figure, like that of tortured Phaethon but larger still.

It is Helios, said Je's disembodied whisper. *Pull him from the flames, restore him to his throne, and* mana *will rain upon the Earth again.*

The flame felt very hot. When Zalazar probed it with his sword, it pushed the swordblade back. "But

what power is this that imprisons him? Je?"

Do not ask questions, mortal. Act.

Zalazar stalked right and left, seeking a way around the flames or through them. The figure inside them did not seem to be burned or tormented by the terrible heat, but only bound. But Zalazar as he approached the tongues of fire had to raise first one hand, and then his shield, to try to protect himself from radiance and glare. The only way to reach the bound god seemed to be to leap directly into the flames, or through them.

Zalazar tried. Unbearable pain seared at him, and the tongues of flame seized him like hands and threw him back. The instant he was clear of the flames, their burning stopped; he was unharmed.

Je shrieked words of compulsion in his ear. Zalazar wrapped himself in his silvery cloak, raised his shield, brandished his sword, and tried again. And was thrown back. And yet again, but all to no avail. And still Je made him try. She stood near now in her full imaged presence.

And yet again the tongues of fire gripped Zalazar, and hurled him flying, sprawling. When Zalazar saw that the metal of his shield was running now in molten drops, he cried aloud his agony: "Spare me, great Je! What will you have from me? Only so much can you make of me, so much and no more."

"I will make whatever I wish of you, mortal. We are so near, so very near to victory!" Her gaze turned to Bormanus, and she went on: "There is a way in which we can augment our power, as I foresaw. Murder will feed great magic."

Zalazar came crawling along the floor, toward the

goddess's feet. He made his hand let go the sword. Only now he realized that no scabbard for it had ever been given him. "Goddess, do not demand of me that I kill my own flesh and blood. It will not bring you victory. I was never a great wizard, even in my youth. No Alhazred, no Vulcan the Shaper. Though even before I met you I had convinced myself of that. A warrior? Conqueror? No, I am not Trillion Mu either, though I have killed; and yours and your demon's power could sustain me in combat for a time even against Thor Red-beard himself. But I cannot do more. Even murder will not give me power enough. And if it could, I will not—"

In fishwife rage, Je lost her self-control. "What are you, thing of clay, to argue with me?" She grabbed Bormanus and forced him forward, bent down so that his neck was exposed for a swordstroke. "Earth is mine to deal with as I will, and you are no more than a clod of earth. Kill him!"

"Destroy me if you will, goddess. If you can. I will not kill him."

Je's eyes glowed, orange fire from a volcano. "I see that I have maddened you with my assistance, until you think you are a demigod at least. You are not worth destruction. If I only withdraw my sustaining power, you will both fall back to earth and be no more than bird-dung when you land. Where will you turn for help if I abandon you?"

Zalazar, on his feet again, turned, physically, looking for help. The half-melted shield now felt impossibly heavy, weighing his left arm down. The brocade of his god-garments hung on him now like lead. The last time the flames had thrown him, some

of their pain had remained in his bones. At a thought from Je, the cloud-floor of the palace would open beneath his feet. He would have a long fall in which to think things over.

The Throne of the World was empty, waiting. No help there. But still he was not going to murder.

Je's voice surprised him in its altered tone. It was less threatening now. "Zalazar, I see that I must tell you the truth. It need not be Helios that you place on the Throne when you have gained the power. It could be me."

"You?"

"The truth is that it could even be yourself."

"I?" Zalazar turned slowly. Looked at the Throne again, and thought, and shook his head. "I am only a poor man, I tell you, goddess. Alone and almost lost. If it is true that I can choose the Ruler of the World, well, it must be some cruel joke, such as you say that even gods are subject to. But if the choice is truly mine to make, I will not give it to you. As for taking it myself, I, I should not. I have no fitness, or powers, or wealth, or even family."

Silence fell in Cloudholm. It was an abrupt change; a stillness that was something more than silence had descended. Zalazar waited, eyes downcast, holding his breath, trying to understand.

Then he began to understand, for the last three words that he himself had spoken seemed to be echoing and re-echoing in the air. All his life he had been a poor nomad with no family at all.

Even the flames of Helios' prison seemed to have cooled somewhat, though Zalazar did not immediately raise his head to look at them. When it seemed to him that the silence might have gone on for half an hour, he did at last look up.

He who had walked with Zalazar as his companion had at last taken the lyre from his belt, and the others were allowed to recognize him now.

Je had recoiled, cringing, herself for once down on one knee, with averted gaze. But Zalazar, for now, could look.

White teeth, inhumanly beautiful and even, smiled at him. "Old man, you have decided well. One comes to claim the Throne in time, and Thanatos will be overcome, and your many-times-great-grandsons will have to choose again; but that is not your problem now. I send you back to Earth. Retain the youth that Je has given you—it is fitting, for a new age of the world has been ordained, though not by me. And memories, if you can, retain them too. Magic must sleep."

Bright, half-melted shield and silver garments fell softly to the floor of cloud, beside the sword. Zalazar was gone.

The bright eyes under the dark curls swept around. The god belted his lyre and unslung his bow. There was a great recessional howling as Je's demon-servant fled, and fell, and fled and fell again.

Je raised her eyes, in a last moment of defiance. The winged head of Hypnos, already hovering beside her ear, silently awaited a command.

"Sleep now, sister Je. As our father Zeus and our brothers and sisters sleep. I join you presently," Apollo said.

Manaspill

Dean Ing

"Keep your head down, Oroles," Thyssa muttered, her face hidden by a fall of chestnut hair. Cross-legged on the moored raft, his lap full of fishnet, little Oroles had forgot his mending in favor of the nearby commotion.

Though the lake was a day's ride end-to-end, it was narrow and shallow. Fisher folk of Lyris traversed it with poled rafts and exchanged rude jokes over the canoe, hewn from an enormous beech, which brought the Moessian dignitary to Lyrian shores. The boy did not answer his sister until the great dugout bumped into place at the nearby wharf, made fast by many hands. "Poo," said Oroles, "foreigners are more fun than mending old Panon's nets. Anyhow, King Bardel doesn't mind me looking."

Thyssa knew that this was so; Lyrians had always regarded their kings with more warmth than awe. Nor would Boerab, the staunch old war minister who stood at the king's left, mind a boy's curiosity. The canoe was very fast, but skittish enough to pitch dignity overboard when dignitaries tried to stand. And what lad could fail to take joy in the sight? Not Oroles!

Yet Thyssa knew also that Minister Dirrach, the shaman standing alert at the young king's right elbow, would interpret a commoner's grin as dumb insolence. "The shaman minds," she hissed. "Do you want to lose favor at the castle?"

©AUSTIN—1981

Grumbling, six-year-old Oroles did as he was told. Thus the boy missed the glance of feral hunger that Dirrach flicked toward the nubile Thyssa before attending to his perquisites as minister to King Bardel of Lyris.

Dirrach seemed barely to sway nearer as he spoke behind young Bardel's ear: "The outlander must not hear you chuckling at his clumsiness, Sire," he suggested in a well-oiled baritone.

Bardel, without moving: "But when I can't laugh, it seems funnier."

"Averae of Moess is devious," the shaman replied easily, while others rushed to help the outlander. "If you think him clumsy, you may falsely think yourself secure."

Bardel gave a grunt of irritation, a sound more mature than his speaking voice. "Dirrach, don't you trust *any*body?"

"I have seen duplicity in that one before," Dirrach murmured, and swayed back to prevent further interchange. Truly enough, he had known Averae before, and had been uneasy when he recognized the Moessian. Dirrach breathed more easily now that he had slandered the man in advance. Who knew what crimes the outlander might recall? Then Averae stood on the wharf, and Bardel stepped forward.

Thyssa had not noted the shaman's glance because her attention was on the king. In the two years since his accession to the Lyrian throne, Bardel had grown into his royal role—indeed, into his father's broad leather breastplate—without entirely losing the panache of spirited youth. Tanned by summer hunts, forearms scarred by combat training with the veteran Boerab, the young Lyrian king fluttered girlish hearts like a warm breeze among beech leaves. And while Bardel watched the Moessian's unsteady advance with calm peregrine eyes, Thyssa saw a twinkle in them. Flanked by Boerab and Dirrach, arms and enchantment, Bardel of Lyris was a beloved figure. It did not matter to most Lyrians that his two ministers loathed each other, and that Bardel was just not awfully bright.

Thyssa, fingers flying among the tattered nets, seemed not to hear the royal amenities. Yet she heard a query from Averae: ". . .Shandorian minister?" And heard Boerab's rumbled, ". . .Escorted from the Northern heights. . .tomorrow." Then Thyssa knew why the castle staff and the fat merchants in Tihan had been atwitter for the past day or so. It could mean nothing less than protracted feasting in Bardel's castle!

To an Achaean of the distant past, or even to Phoenicians who plied the Adriatic coast to the far Southwest, this prospect would have inspired little awe. No Lyrian commoner could afford woven garments for everyday use; only the king and Boerab carried iron blades at their sides, each weapon purchased from Ostran ironmongers with packtrains of excellent Lyrian wine.

Nor would the royal castle in Tihan have excited much admiration from those legendary outlanders. Some hundreds of families lived in Tihan, thatched walls and roofs protected by stout oak palisades surrounding town and castle on the lake's one peninsula. Bardel's castle was the only two-story structure capacious enough to house king, staff, and a small

garrison mostly employed for day-labor.

The pomp that accompanied Bardel's retinue back to nearby Tihan would have brought smiles to Phoenician lips but as Thyssa viewed the procession, her eyes were bright with pride. "Remind me to brush your leather apron, Oroles," she smiled; "if you are chosen to serve during feast-time, there may be red meat for our stew." Unsaid was her corollary: *and since I must play both father and mother to you, perhaps I too will make an impression on someone.*

* * * *

Old Panon was less than ecstatic over the job on his nets. "Your repairs are adequate, Thyssa," he admitted, then held an offending tangle between thumb and forefinger; "but Oroles must learn that a knot needn't be the size and shape of a clenched fist. Teach him as I taught you, girl; nothing magic about it."

"Nothing?" Oroles frowned at this heresy. "But Shaman Dirrach enchants the nets every year."

"Pah," said the old man. "Dirrach! The man couldn't—ah, there are those who say the man couldn't enchant a bee with honey. Some say it's all folderol to keep us in line. *Some* say," he qualified it.

"Please, Panon," said Thyssa, voice cloudy with concern. "Big-eared little pitchers, "she ruffled the ragged hair of Oroles, "spill on everyone. Besides, if it's folderol how do you explain my father's slingstone?"

"Well,—" The old man smiled, "maybe some small magics. It doesn't take much enchantment to fool a fish, or a rabbit. And Urkut *was* an uncanny marksman with a sling."

At this, Oroles beamed. The boy had no memory of the mother who had died bearing him, and chiefly second-hand knowledge of his emigrant father, Urkut. But the lad had spent many an evening scrunched next to the fireplace, hugging his knees and wheedling stories from Thyssa as she stirred chestnuts from the coals. To the girl, a father who had seen the Atlantic and Crete had traveled all the world. One raised across the mountains beyond Lyris was an emigrant. And one whose slingstone was so unerring that the missile was kept separate in Urkut's waistpouch, was definitely magical. Indeed, the day before his death Urkut had bested Dirrach by twice proving the incredible efficacy of his sling. It had come about during an aurochs hunt in which Bardel, still an impressionable youth, and Boerab, an admirer of Urkut, had been spectators.

As Thyssa heard it from the laconic Boerab, her father's tracking skill had prompted young Bardel to proclaim him "almost magical." Dirrach, affronted, had caused a grass fire to appear behind them; though Boerab left little doubt that he suspected nothing more miraculous in the shaman's ploy than a wisp of firewick from Dirrach's pack. Challenged to match the grass fire, Urkut had demurred until goaded by Bardel's amusement.

Slowly (as Thyssa would embroider it, matching her account with remembered pantomime while gooseflesh crawled on Oroles's body), the hunter Urkut had withdrawn a rough stone pellet from his wallet. Carefully, standing in wooden stirrups while his pony danced in uncertainty, Urkut had placed pellet in slingpouch. Deliberately, staring into

Dirrach's face as he whirled the sling, Urkut had made an odd gesture with his free hand. And then the stone had soared off, not in a flat arrowcourse but in a high trajectory to thud far off behind a shrub.

Dirrach's booming laughter had stopped abruptly when, dismounting at the shrub, Urkut groped and then held his arms aloft. In one hand he'd held his slingstone. In the other had been a rabbit.

Outraged by Dirrach's claims of charlatanry, Urkut had done it again; this time eyes closed, suggesting that Boerab retrieve stone and quarry.

And this time Boerab had found a magnificent cock pheasant quivering beside the slingstone, and Urkut had sagaciously denied any miraculous powers while putting his slingstone away. It was merely a trick, he'd averred; the magic of hand and eye (this with a meaningful gaze toward Dirrach). And young Bardel had bidden Urkut sup at the castle that night. And Urkut had complied.

And Urkut had died in his cottage during the night, in agony, clutching his belly as Thyssa wept over him. To this day, even Dirrach would admit that the emigrant Urkut had been in some small way a shaman. *Especially* Dirrach; for he could also point out that mana was lethal to those who could not control it properly.

Now, with a sigh for memories of a time when she was not an orphan, Thyssa said to the aged Panon: "Father always said the mana was in the slingstone, not in him. And it must have been true, for the pellet vanished like smoke after his death."

"Or so the shaman says," Panon growled. "He who took charge of Urkut's body and waistpouch as well.

I heard, Thyssa. And I watch Dirrach—almost as carefully as *he* watches *you*." The fisherman chose two specimens from his catch; one suitable for a stew, the other large enough to fillet. "Here: an Oroles'-worth, and a Thyssa-worth."

The girl thanked him with a hug, gathered the fish in her leather shift, leapt from raft to shore with a flash of lithe limbs. "May you one day catch a Panon-worth," she called gaily, and took the hand of Oroles.

"He watches you, girl," old Panon's voice followed her toward the palisades of Tihan. "Take care." She waved and continued. Dirrach watched everybody, she told herself. What special interest could the shaman possibly have in an orphaned peasant girl?

*   *   *   *

There were some who could have answered Thyssa's riddle. One such was the gaunt emissary Averae, whose dignity had been in such peril as he stood up in his Moessian canoe. Not until evening, after an aurochs haunch had been devoured and a third flagon of Lyrian wine was in his vitals, did Averae unburden himself to Boerab. "You could've knocked me into the lake when I spied your friend, the shaman," Averae muttered.

"Or a falling leaf could've," Boerab replied with a wink. "You're a landlubber like me. But be cautious in naming my friends," he added with a sideways look across the table where Dirrach was tongue-lashing a servant.

"You've no liking for him either?"

"I respect his shrewdness. We serve the same king," Boerab said with a lift of the heavy shoulders. "You know Dirrach, then?"

"When your king was only a pup—I mean no disrespect for him, Boerab, but this marvelous wine conjures truth as it will—his father sent Dirrach to us in Moess to discuss fishing rights near our shore."

"I was building an outpost and only heard rumors."

"Here are facts. Dirrach had full immunity, royal pardons, the usual," Averae went on softly, pausing to drain his flagon. "And he abused them terribly among our servant girls."

"You mean the kind of abuse he's giving now?" An ashen-faced winebearer was backing away from Dirrach.

A weighed pause: "I mean the kind that leaves bite scars, and causes young women to despise all men."

Boerab, a heavy womanizer in his time, saw no harm in a tussle with a willing wench. But bite scars? The old warrior recalled the disappearance of several girls from farms near Tihan over the past years, and hoped he could thrust a new suspicion from his mind. "Well, that explains why we never arranged that fishing treaty," he said, trying to smile. "Perhaps this time Lyris and Moess can do better."

"Trade from Obuda to the Phoenician coast is more important than punishment for a deviate," Averae agreed. "Do you suppose we'll find Shandor's folk amenable?"

"Likely; they have little to lose and much to gain."

"Even as you and I," Averae purred the implication.

"Even as your king and mine," Boerab corrected. "Just so we'll understand one another, Averae: I'm happy as I am. Wouldn't know what to do with presents from Moess or Shandor, even without strings attached. If Lyris and the lad—ah, King Bardel—prosper, I'm content."

"Fair enough," Averae laughed. "I'm beginning to be glad your mana was strong during our border clash."

Boerab, startled, spilled his brimming flagon. "My *what*? Save that for commoners, Averae."

"If you insist. But it's common knowledge in Moess that our shaman spent the better part of his mana trying to sap your strength in that last battle. Practically ruined the poor fellow."

Boerab studied the lees in his wine. "If anybody put a wardspell on me, he's kept it secret." The barrel chest shook with mirth. "Fact is, I had high-ground advantage and grew too tired to move. If you want to believe, then believe in a safespot. For myself, I believe in my shield."

Boerab could hardly be blamed for denying the old legends. The entire region was rich in relics of forgotten battles where mighty shamans had pitted spell against spell, mana against mana, irresistible ax versus immovable shield. The mound that Boerab had chosen for his stand was a natural choice for a combat veteran; other warriors had chosen that spot before him. On that spot, magical murder had been accomplished. On that spot no magic would work again, ever. Boerab had indeed defended a safespot upon which all but the most stupendous mana was wasted.

All Boerab's life had been spent in regions nearly exhausted of mana. Of course there had been little things like Urkut's tricks, but—. Boerab did not commit the usual mistake of allowing magic to explain the commonplace. Instead he erred in using the commonplace to explain magic. Thus far, Boerab was immeasurably far ahead.

"I'd drink to your shield, then," Averae mumbled, "if that confounded winebearer were in sight."

Boerab's eyes roamed through the smog of the lignite fire as he roared for more wine. By now the king and Dirrach were too far in their flagons to notice the poor service. Boerab promised himself that for the main feast, he'd insist on a winebearer too young to crave the stuff he toted. *Ah; Urkut's boy,* he thought. *Too innocent to cause aggravation.*

As to the innocence of Oroles, the grizzled warrior was right. As to the consequences of innocence he could scarcely have gone farther wrong.

*   *   *   *

Thyssa, late to rise, was coaxing a glow from hardwood embers when she heard a rap on her door. "Welcome," she called, drawing her shift about her as the runner, Dasio, entered.

"In the royal service," said Dasio formally. The youth was lightly built but tall, extraordinary in musculature of calf and thigh; and Thyssa noted the heaving breast of her childhood friend with frank concern.

"Are you ill, Dasio? You cannot be winded by a mere sprint across Tihan."

"Nor am I. I'm lathered from a two-hour run. Spent the night with the Shandorians; they'll be here soon—with a surprise, I'll warrant," Dasio said cryptically, taking his eyes from Thyssa with reluctance. Seeing Oroles curled in a tangle of furs: "Ah, there's the cub I'm to fetch; and then I can rest!"

Choosing a motherly view, Thyssa set a stoneware pot near the coals. "Tell them Oroles was breaking his fast," she said. "You don't have to tell them you shared his gruel. Meanwhile, Dasio, take your ease." She shook her small brother with rough affection. "Rise, little man-of-the-house," she smiled. "You're wanted—" and glanced at Dasio as she ended, "—at the castle?"

The runner nodded, stirred the gruel as it began to heat, tasted and grimaced. "Wugh; it could use salt."

"Could it indeed," Thyssa retorted. "Then you might have brought some. Our palates aren't so jaded with rich palace food as some I might name."

A flush crept up the neck of the diffident youth. Silently he chided himself; though Thyssa and Oroles still lived in Urkut's cottage, they did so with few amenities. Without even the slenderest dowry, Dasio knew, the girl was overlooked by the sons of most Tihaners.

Presently, Oroles found his sandals and apron, then joined Dasio over the gruel. "What have I done now," he yawned.

It was as Thyssa hoped. After one dutiful mouthful that courtesy required, Dasio set her at ease. "The palace cook will brief you, runt. Big doings tonight; bigger than last night. If you can keep your feet untangled, maybe you can ask for a slab of salt—to jade your palates," he added with a sidelong grin at Thyssa.

Moments later, the girl ushered them outside. "Watch over him, Dasio," she pleaded. "And thanks for his employ."

"Thank old Boerab for that," said the youth. "But I'll try to keep the cub out of the wine he'll pour tonight." Then, while Oroles tried to match his stride, Dasio trotted slowly up the dirt road toward high ground and the castle.

*   *   *   *

The Shandorians arrived in midafternoon, and all Tihan buzzed with the surprise Dasio had promised. Everybody knew Shandor had funny ideas about women, but conservative Tihaners grumbled to see that the emissary from Shandor was a handsome female wearing crimson garments of the almost mythical fabric, silk; and her eyes were insolent with assurance. Thyssa, contracting a day's labor for a parcel of a merchant's grain, knew it first as rumor.

Dirrach learned of it while powdering a lump of lightest-tinted lignite coal in his private chamber. It was the shaman's good fortune that such stuff was available, since when powdered it was unlikely to be as visible when sprinkled from shadow into fire as was charcoal or the sulphur which he used for other effects. It was the region's good fortune that Dirrach's "magics" had never yet tapped genuine mana.

Dirrach heard his door creak open; turned to hide his work even as he opened his mouth to blast the intruder. Only one man in all Lyris had the right to burst in thus. "Who dares to— oh. Ah, welcome, Bardel," he ended lamely; for it was that one man.

"Can you believe, Dirrach?" The king's face was awash with something between delight and consternation as he toed the door shut. "Boerab and I just did the welcomes—and where were you anyhow— oh, here I guess; and the Shandorian has a girl for a

servant. Which is fine I suppose, because she's a woman. The emissary, I mean. Is a *woman!*"

Dirrach drew a long breath, moving away from his work to draw Bardel's attention. Too long had he suffered the prattle, the presumption, the caprice of this royal oaf. Perhaps tonight, all that could be remedied. "Shandor puts undue value on its females, as I have told you." He hadn't, but Bardel's shortsword outspanned his memory.

"The Shandorian's a bit long in the tooth for me," Bardel went on, "but firm-fleshed and—uh—manly, sort of. But where do we seat a woman at a state feast? You take care of it, Dirrach; Boerab's rounded up the kitchen staff. I'm off to the practice range; that crazy Gethae—the Shandorian—would pit her skill with a bow against mine. A woman, Dirrach," he laughed, shaking his head as he ducked out the door. His parting question was his favorite phrase: "Can you *believe?*"

Dirrach sighed and returned to his work. No believer in the arts he surrogated, the shaman warmed to his own beliefs. He could believe in careful preparation in the feast hall, and in mistrust for outlanders who could be blamed for any tragedy. Most of all, Dirrach could believe in poison. The stuff had served him well in the past.

*   *   *   *

Dirrach's seating arrangements were clever, the hanging oil lamps placed so that he would be partly in shadow near the fireplace. The special flagstone rested atop the bladder where Dirrach's foot could reach it, and specially decorated flagons bore symbols that clearly implied who would sit where. The shaman's duties included tasting every course and flagon before it reached the royal lips, though poison was little used in Lyris. Dirrach congratulated himself on placing the woman across from him, for Dirrach's place was at the king's side, and anything the woman said to Bardel could be noted by the shaman as well. A second advantage was that women were widely known to have scant capacity for wine; Gethae would sit at the place most likely to permit unmasking of a shaman's little tricks; and if Gethae denounced him it could be chalked up to bleary vision of an inebriate who could also be accused of hostile aims. Especially on the morrow.

Yet Gethae showed herself to good advantage as she swept into the castle with her new acquaintances. "I claim a rematch," she said, laying a companionable hand on Boerab's shoulder gorget. "Bardel's eye is a trifle too good today." Her laugh was throaty, her carriage erect and, Dirrach admitted, almost kingly. Already she spoke Bardel's name with ease.

Bardel started to enter the hall, stumbled as he considered letting the stately Gethae precede him but reconsidered in the same instant that such courtesy was reserved for the mothers of kings. "I was lucky, Gethae—ooop, damn flagstones anyhow; ahh, smells good in here; oh, *there* you are, Dirrach," Bardel rattled on with a wave. Actually the hall stank of smoke and sweat—but then, so did the king.

Boerab introduced Dirrach to the Shandorian whom he treated as an equal. "Sorry you were busy here, Dirrach," the old soldier lied manfully. "This sturdy wench pulls a stronger bow than I thought possible."

"Put it down to enthusiasm," said Gethae, exchanging handclasps with Dirrach. Her glance was both calculating and warm.

"Huh; put it down to good pectorals," Boerab rejoined, then raised his eyes to heaven: "Ulp; ghaaaa. . ."

"I accept that as a compliment," said Gethae, smiling.

Dirrach saw that such compliments were justified; the Shandorian's physical impact could not be denied, and a man like Boerab might find his judgment colored with lust. But Dirrach's tastes were narrow and, "I fear we have prepared but rough entertainment for a lady," said the shaman in cool formality.

"I can accept that too," she said, still smiling as she peered at the feast table. "Ho, Averae: I see we're to be kept apart."

Averae of Moess found his own place with a good-natured gibe to the effect that a small plot with Shandor would have been a pleasure. Plainly, the shaman saw, this woman enjoyed the company of men without considering herself one. Had he only imagined an invitation in her smile of greeting?

Dirrach found that it had not been mere imagination. All through the courses of chestnut bread, beef and fowl, beer and honeycake, the shaman shifted his feet to avoid the questing instep of the long-legged Gethae. At one point Dirrach felt his false-bottomed flagstone sink as he hastily moved his foot, saw reflection in Gethae's frank dark eyes of a sudden flare in the fireplace. But Gethae was stoking a fire of another sort and noticed nothing but Dirrach himself. The shaman took it philosophically; he could not help it if Gethae had an appetite for men in their middle years. But he would not whet that appetite either, and pointedly guided Bardel into dialogue with the woman.

Eventually the beer was replaced by a tow-headed lad bearing the most famed product of Lyris: the heady wine of the north lakeshore. Gethae sipped, smacked, grinned; sipped again. Very soon she pronounced her flagon empty and beamed at the boy who filled it. "The lad," she said to one and all, "has unlocked Lyris's wealth!"

All took this as a toast and Gethae winked at the boy, who winked back. "I predict you'll go far,—ah, what's your name, lad?"

"Oroles, ma'am," said the boy, growing restive as others turned toward the interchange. "I've already gone as far as the end of the lake."

"You'll go farther," Gethae chuckled.

"Here's to travel," said the king. "Keep traveling around the table, Orolandes."

Dutiful laughter faded as the boy replied; servants did not correct kings. "Oroles, please sir—but you're almost right."

Boerab, in quick jocularity: "In honor of the great Orolandes, no doubt."

"Aw, you knew that, Boerab," said the boy in gentle accusation, and again filled Gethae's flagon, his tongue between his teeth as he poured. The boy's innocent directness, his ignorance of protocol, his serious mien struck warm response first from Averae, himself a grandfather. Averae began to chuckle, then to laugh outright as others joined in.

Little Oroles did not fathom this levity and continued in his rounds until, perceiving that his own king was laughing at him, he stopped, hugging the wine pitcher to him. The small features clouded; a single tear ran down his cheek.

Boerab was near enough to draw Oroles to him, to offer his flagon for filling, to mutter in the boy's ear. "No fear, lad; they're laughing for you, not at you."

Bethae could not tell whether Boerab was praising or scolding the boy and resolved to generate a diversion. With a by-your-leave to Bardel she stood. "At such a merry moment, a guest might choose to pay tribute."

"Ill-said," from Averae, "because I wish I'd said it first." More merriment, fueled by alcohol.

"I yield," Gethae mimed a fetching swoon, "to Moess—for once."

Bardel understood enough of this byplay to lead the guffaws. Averae bowed to the king, to the woman, then performed quick syncopated handclaps before turning expectantly toward the door.

A blocky Moessian—it was poor form to seat one's bodyguard at a state feast—entered, arms outstretched with obvious effort to hold their burden. At Averae's gesture, the man knelt before the beaming young king.

"May you never need to use it, sire," from Averae.

Bardel took the wicked handax, licked its cold iron head to assure himself of its composition. It was a heavy cast Ostran head, hafted with care, and as Bardel swung it experimentally the applause was general.

Except for Dirrach. The shaman muttered something unintelligible and Bardel's face fell. "This

pleased me so," said the king, "that I forgot. Trust Dirrach to remind me: no weapons in the feast hall. No, no, Averae," he said quickly; "you gave no offense. Boy," he offered the ax to Oroles, "have a guard put this in my chamber. I'll sleep with it tonight."

So it shall be mine tomorrow, thought Dirrach.

Oroles, cradling the wine pitcher in one arm, took the ax with his free hand. Its weight caused him nearly to topple, a splash of golden liquid cascading onto the flagstones. Dirrach was not agile enough and, wine-splattered to his knees, would have struck the boy who bolted from the hall with wine and weapon.

But: "A boy for a man's job," Boerab tutted. "At least we have wine to waste."

Dirrach quenched his outward anger, resumed his seat and said innocently, "I fear we have given offense to Moess." He knew the suggestion would be remembered on the morrow, despite Averae's denial which was immediate and cordial.

Then it was Gethae's turn. The Shandorian reached into her scarlet silken sleeve, produced a sueded pouch, offered it to Bardel with a small obeisance.

"What else might Shandorians have up their sleeves," murmured Dirrach with false bonhomie.

"A body search might reward you," Gethae replied in open invitation. Dirrach did not need to respond for at that moment Bardel emptied the pouch into his hand. There was total silence.

"Oh damn," Gethae breathed, and chuckled; "I'd hoped to keep them damp." Bardel, perplexed, held several opaque porous stones. One, by far the largest, was the size of a goose egg, set into a horn bezel hung from a finely braided leather loop. The others were unset and all had been smoothed to the texture of eggshell.

Dirrach almost guessed they were gallstones, for which magical properties were sometimes claimed. Instead he kept a wise look, and his silence.

Gethae retrieved the great stone. "Here; a bit of magic from the northern barbarians, if you'll stretch a point." She extended her tongue, licked the stone which actually adhered to the moist flesh until she plucked it away, held it aloft. Even Dirrach gasped.

The properties of hydrophane opal were unknown even in Shandor; Gethae had been jesting about magic. The Shandorians had imported the stones from the north at tremendous expense; knew only that this most porous of opals was dull when dry but became a glittering pool of cloudy luminescence when dampened. As the moisture evaporated, the stone would again become lackluster. Thus the Shandorians did not suspect the enormous concentration of mana which was unlocked by moistening a hydrophane.

Had Gethae known the proper spell, she could have carved away the Tihan peninsula or turned it all to metal with the power she held. Even her fervent prayer for strength to pull a Lyrian bow had been enough earlier, before the opals in her pouch had dried. Yet none of this was suspected by Gethae. Her fluid gesture in returning the huge gem to Bardel was half of a stormspell. She, with the others present, interpreted the sudden skin-prickling electricity in the air as the product of awe.

Bardel took the gift in wonderment. "Spit is magic?"

"Or water, wine, perspiration," Gethae chuckled. "I have heard it argued that oil scum on water creates the same illusion of magical beauty. And has the same natural explanation," she shrugged. "Don't ask me to explain it; merely accept it as Shandor's gift."

This called for another toast. "Where the devil is that winebearer?" Bardel asked.

Oroles scurried back from his errand to pour. Even Bardel could see the boy trembling in anticipation of punishment, saw too that the outlanders had taken a liking to the slender child. With wisdom rare in him, Bardel suddenly picked up the smallest of the opals, still opaque and dry. The king ostentatiously dipped the pebble into his wine, held it up before Oroles who marveled silently at the transformation. "For your services," said Bardel, "and for entertainment." With that he dropped the opal, the size of a babe's thumbnail, into the hand of Oroles.

Bardel acknowledged the applause, hung the great hydrophane amulet around his own sweaty neck, pledged packtrains of Lyrian wine as gifts for Moess and Shandor. "And what say you of outlander magics," he asked of the glum Dirrach. It was as near as Bardel would come to commanding a performance from his shaman. He knew some doubted Dirrach's miracles, but Bardel was credulous as any bumpkin.

Dirrach grasped his talisman of office, a carved wand with compartmented secrets of its own, and waved it in the air. "Iron strikes fire on stone," he intoned; "stone holds inner fire with water. But true mana can bring fire to fire itself." It only sounded silly, he told himself, if you thought about it. But the powdered lignite in the wand would keep anybody else from thinking about it.

Dirrach knew where the fireplace was, did not need to look over his shoulder as he manipulated the wand and trod on the false flagstone, feeding pungent oil to the blaze. He felt the heat, saw astonishment in the eyes of his audience, smiled to see Oroles cringe against the wall. He did not realize that the flames behind him had, for a moment only, blazed *black*. The gleaming hydrophanes of Bardel and Oroles were near enough that Dirrach's wandpass had called forth infinitesimal mana in obedience to a reversal gesture-spell. It did not matter that Dirrach was wholly incompetent to command mana. All that mattered was the mana and the many means for its discharge as magic. Knowingly or not. The jewel at Bardel's throat glimmered with unspent lightnings.

Unaware of the extent of his success, and of the enormous forces near him, Dirrach mixed blind luck with his sleight-of-hand and his hidden-lever tricks. The shaman was a bit flummoxed when two white doves fluttered up from the false bottom of his carven chair; he'd only put one bird in there. He was similarly pensive when the coin he "found" in Averae's beard turned out to be, not the local bronze celt Dirrach had palmed beforehand, but a silvery roundish thing which Averae claimed before either of them got a good look at the picture stamped on it. Inspection would have told them little in any case: the Thracian portrait of Alexander was not due to be reproduced for centuries to come.

And when a spatter of rain fell inside, all assumed that it was also raining *out*side; even royal roofs leaked a bit. At last Gethae sighed, "My compliments, Dirrach. But tell me: how did you breed mice to elk? That was subtly done."

Indeed it was; so subtly that only Gethae had noticed the tiny antlered creatures that scampered across hearthstones and into the fire during one of Dirrach's accidental spells. Dirrach did not know if his leg was being pulled, and only smiled.

Bardel called for more wine when the shaman claimed his mana was waning. Oroles was pouring when Averae asked what credence might be placed in the tales of ancient shamans.

"Much of it is true," replied Dirrach, taking an obligatory sip from Bardel's flagon, thinking he lied even as he gazed at the truth gleaming darkly on Bardel's breast. "Yet few of us know the secrets today. You'd be surprised what silly frauds I've seen; and as for the nonsense I hear from afar: well—" Aping a lunatic's expression, hands fluttering like his doves, Dirrach began a ludicrous capering that brought on gales of mirth. And while his audience watched the wand he tossed into the air, Dirrach dropped a pinch of death into the king's flagon. There was enough poison there to dispatch a dozen Bardels. Dirrach would feign illness presently, and of course the winebearer would later be tortured for information he did not have.

But there was information which Dirrach lacked, as well. He would never have performed a gestural wardspell, nor given anyone but himself the gift of conversing with other species, had he known just what occult meanings lay in his mummery.

*　　*　　*　　*

The next day was one of sweltering heat, and did nothing to sweeten the odor of the fish Thyssa was filleting outside Panon's smokehouse. "Oroles, turn these entrails under the soil in Panon's garden," she called. "Oroles!"

The boy dropped his new treasure into his waist-pouch, hopped from his perch on a handcart and scrambled to comply after muttering something, evidently to thin air.

"Don't complain," she said, tasting perspiration on her lips.

"I wasn't," said Oroles. "Did you know the castle midden heap is rich with last night's leavings and, uh, suc—succulent mice?"

"How would you know," she asked, not really listening.

"Oh—something just tells me."

Despite her crossness, Thyssa smiled. "A little bird, no doubt."

Pausing to consider: "That's an idea," the boy said, and trudged off, head averted from his burden.

Hidden from Thyssa by the smokehouse, Oroles could still be heard as he distributed fish guts in the garden. "Don't take it all," he said. "I'm supposed to plant this stuff." Thyssa thought she heard the creak of an old hinge, clucking, snapping. "No I'm not; you're talking people-talk," Oroles went on. More creaking. No, not a hinge. What, then? "There's a ferret under the cart that can do it too. Funny I never noticed it before." Creak, pop. "All right, if you promise not to steal grain."

There was more, but Thyssa first investigated the cart. A dark sinuous shape streaked away nearly underfoot to find refuge in Panon's woodpile; there *had* been a ferret hiding there! Thyssa crept to the edge of the smokehouse, spied Oroles dividing his offal between the dirt and a raven that was half as large as he. Neither seemed to fear the other. If she hadn't known better, Thyssa would have sworn the two were actually exchanging the polite gossip of new acquaintances. But the boy didn't seem to be in danger, and he had few enough playmates. Thyssa tiptoed back to her work, waved the flies away, and chose another fish from the pile.

Presently Oroles returned, searched around the cart, then began to string fillets onto withes. "I wonder if the shaman is sick in the head," he said.

"Not he," Thyssa laughed. "Why would you think that?"

"He keeps squatting at his window, running back to leap into bed when servants appear, going back to the window,—you know," Oroles said vaguely.

Dirrach's chamber upstairs in the castle faced the dawn, away from Panon's cottage. Oroles would have had to climb a tree to see such goings-on. "Your little bird told you," said Thyssa.

"Quite a big one," Oroles insisted, as a raven flapped away overhead. Thyssa felt the boy's forehead. Such behavior was not at all usual for Oroles.

* * * *

Dirrach did not step outside his chamber until he spotted Bardel near the vineyards with the outlanders. The shaman had retired from the feast with complaints of a gripe in his belly, fully expecting to wake to the sweet music of lamentations from servants. Told of Bardel's vineyard tour, Dirrach suspected a ruse; continued to fake his illness; told himself that Boerab must go next. Dirrach *knew* the poison had gone into the flagon, had seen Bardel swill it down.

Maybe the fool had thrown it all up soon after Dirrach took his leave. Yes, that had to be the answer. The only other possibility was some inexplicable miracle. Well, there were other paths to regicide. One path would have to be chosen while the outlanders were still available as suspects.

At the noon meal, the king glowed with health and camaraderie. "Try some more stew, Dirrach; just the thing to settle your innards."

"Aye, and to bank your fires for negotiations," Gethae put in. "Bardel wouldn't hear of serious talk while you were indisposed."

"Bardel was nearly indisposed himself, this morning," Averae grunted. Noting Dirrach's sudden interest, he continued: "Set your entrails right before your king runs out of luck."

Boerab grunted at this understatement; but courtesy forbade outright mention of a king's death. "Made me dizzy to watch him, Dirrach; climbing like a squirrel to fetch grapes that were still unripe."

A king, engaged in such foolishness! Dirrach's face mirrored the thought.

"It wasn't the climb that impressed me, so much as the fall," Gethae said, her hand tracing the tumble of a falling leaf. She went on to describe Bardel's acrobatic ascent, the gleam of the hydrophane on his breast as he sweated to the topmost extent of a vine high in a beechtree.

Bardel, deluded that such childish heroics made the right impression: "I don't think I missed a branch on the way down."

"Brought enough of them down with you," Boerab snorted. "What a thump you made!"

Dirrach picked at his food, wondering how much of the tale was decoration. Taking it at half its face value, Bardel should now be lying in state—and in a basket, at that.

From Gethae: "I've never seen better evidence of a wardspell."

At this, Bardel thanked his shaman for his coronation wardspell, now several years old and, in any case, known by Dirrach to be pure counterfeit. Or was it? Dirrach silently enumerated the scars and bruises sustained by Bardel since the coronation; rejected his wardspell out of hand. Still, something was accountable for a flurry of bizarre events—and all since the previous evening. Was the woman teasing him with covert hints? Dirrach allowed himself to wonder if one of the outlanders was a true shaman, and felt his flesh creep. Forewarned, a wise man would take careful note of further anomalies.

Mindful of royal duties, anxious to show himself equal to them in the very near future, Dirrach suggested a brief attendance to local matters before the open-ended negotiations. While emissaries lounged at one end of the chamber, Bardel settled several complaints from citizens of Tihan and vicinity. The runner, Dasio, rounded up petitioners quickly—all but one, for whom Dasio had promised to plead.

When a squabble between farmers had been concluded, Bardel stood up. "Is that the last, runner?"

"Yes, sire, . . ."

"Well then, . . ."

"And no, sire," Dasio said quickly. "I mean, there is one small matter, but of great import to the girl, Thyssa." Dasio saw the king's impatience, felt the cold stare of Dirrach. Yet he had promised, and: "She begs the special attention of the shaman but dared not leave her work to make petition."

Bardel sat back in obvious pique. Dirrach opened his mouth to deny the petition; remembered the visitors. "Quickly then," he said.

"The girl fears for her brother, Oroles. She thinks he is suddenly possessed; and truly, the cub is not himself. Thyssa craves audience with our wise shaman, and is prepared to pay in menial labor."

"Thyssa? Oh, the daughter of Urkut," Bardel said.

Dirrach's eyes gleamed as he recalled the girl. Prepared to do services for him, was she? But time enough for that when Dirrach occupied the throne. "Next week, perhaps," he muttered to Bardel.

"But her brother was the pup I rewarded last eve," Bardel mused. "He seemed only too normal then. What exactly is his trouble?"

Alarms clamored in Dirrach's mind as Dasio blurted, "He thinks he talks with animals, sire. And in truth, it seems that he does!"

The shaman leaned, muttered into the royal ear. "The shaman will make compassionate treatment before this day is done," Bardel said, parroting what echoed in his ear. So saying, he concluded the session.

*　　　*　　　*　　　*

Following Dasio to the girl's cottage, Dirrach applauded himself for the delay he had caused in negotiations. The outlander runners, in search of boundary clarification, would need three days for round trips to Shandor and Moess. In that time, a crafty shaman might learn more of these evidences of true occult power and perhaps even circumvent the luck of a king.

Dasio had alerted Thyssa to expect the shaman; traded worried glances with her as Dirrach strode into the cottage. Dirrach waited until the girl and Oroles had touched foreheads to his sandal before bidding Dasio leave them.

"The boy knows why I come?" Dirrach kept the edge off his voice, the better to interrogate them. The more he looked on Thyssa, the more honeyed his tones became.

Thyssa had told the boy, who rather enjoyed his sudden celebrity. "He's never acted this way before," she said, wringing her hands, "and I thought perhaps some fever—."

Dirrach made a few stately passes in the air. A faint chittering reached them from outside. The opal of Oroles nestled in the boy's waistpouch unseen and, somewhere in the distance, a dog howled in terror. Kneeling, Dirrach took the boy's arms, then his hands, in his own. No trembling, no fever, no perspiration; only honest dirt. "His fever is in his bones, and will subside," Dirrach lied, then pointed to a cricket at the hearth. "What does the insect say, boy?"

"Bugs don't say much, 'cause they don't know much," was the prompt reply. "I tried earlier; they just say the same things: warm, cold, hungry, scared —you know. Bugs ain't smart."

"How about mice?"

"A little smarter. What does 'horny' mean?"

Dirrach would have shared a knowing smile with Thyssa, but saw her acute discomfort. To Oroles he said, "It seems that your ability comes and goes."

"It went today while I was working under Panon's raft. You have to strip and swim under. You know those baitfish he keeps alive in a basket? Not a word," Oroles said in wonderment.

Dirrach persisted. The boy showed none of the fear or caution of a small boy perpetrating a large fraud; but to ensure Dirrach of the sister's pliant services, Oroles must seem to be mending. The shaman hinted broadly that cubs who lied about mana could expect occult retribution, adding, "Besides, no one would believe you."

Oroles said stolidly, "You would. A raven told me he watched you running to and fro from your bed to your window this morning."

"The raven lied," Dirrach said quickly, feeling icy centipedes on his spine.

"And the ferret is angry because Dasio is standing between him and a rat nest, right outside."

Dirrach flung open the door. In the dusk he saw Dasio patiently waiting nearby, his feet less than a pace away from a well-gnawed hole in the foundation wattling. No sign of a ferret—but then, there wouldn't be. Dirrach contained a mounting excitement, sent the girl away with Dasio, and began testing the boy further. Though lacking clear concepts of experimental controls, the shaman knew that he must verify the events, then isolate the conditions in which they occurred.

An hour later, Dirrach stood at lakeside with a shivering and very wet Oroles, smiling at the boy. He no longer doubted the gift of Oroles; had traced its mana first to clothing, then to waistpouch, finally to proximity of Oroles with the tiny stone in the pouch. Such knowledge, of course, must not be shared.

Teeth chattering, Oroles tugged his leather breechclout on and fingered his waistpouch. "Can I have my gleamstone back?"

"A pretty bauble," said Dirrach, eyeing its moonlit glitter; "but quite useless."

"Then why can't I have it back?"

Dirrach hesitated. The boy would complain if his treasure were taken, and no breath of its importance could be tolerated. If the boy should drown now? But too many people would wonder at Dirrach's peculiar ministrations. Ah: there were other, larger stones; one of which just might explain much of young Bardel's escapes from death. Imperiously: "Take the gleamstone, cub; I can get all of them I want."

"The raven told you, I bet," Oroles teased.

Dirrach led the boy back to the cottage, subtly leading the conversation where he willed. Before taking his leave, he learned that Oroles's winged crony had admired the gleamstone, had claimed to know where a great many of them could be found near a warm spring in the northern mountains. It was not difficult to frighten the lad into silence, and to enlist him in the effort to locate a spring whose warm waters might have curative power. Dirrach returned to the castle in good spirits that night, resolved to keep his curtains drawn in the future.

*　　*　　*　　*

After a dull morning spent on details of safe-passage agreements, the outlanders were amenable to an afternoon's leisure. They groaned inwardly at Bardel's proposal, but the deer hunt was quickly arranged. Dirrach would have preferred to wait in Tihan, the sooner to hear what his small conspirator might learn of the thermal spring; but the shaman had been absent from state affairs too much already; who knew what friendships Bardel might nurture with outlanders in the interim? Dirrach's fingers itched for a mana-rich hydrophane; the sooner he could experiment with them, the better for him. The worse for others.

A series of small things suggested to Dirrach that the great stone at Bardel's throat was constantly active. When Boerab stood in his stirrups by the king's side and waved their beaters toward a ridge, both men found themselves unhorsed comically. They cursed the groom whose saddle knots had slipped, but it was Dirrach's surmise—a lucky guess—that knot-loosening spells were easy ones, even by accident. Far better, Dirrach thought, if he could surreptitiously try spells while within arm's reach of Bardel —but the king was much too alert and active during a hunt, and at the negotiation table such incantatory acts would be even more obvious. And always the shaman kept one eye on the winged motes that swept the sky, and thought of ravens.

The hunt was not a total loss for Dirrach, who cozened a wager from his king early in the afternoon. "One of the Shandorian gems, is it?" Bardel laughed.

"Fair enough! If I can't capture my quarry intact, a stone is yours."

"But if he does, Dirrach, you have an iron axhead to hone," Boerab grinned. "Bit of honest labor would do you no harm," and the warrior rode off with his king.

The deer they surprised in the small ravine amounted almost to a herd. His foolhardiness growing by the minute, Bardel was in his glory. His shaggy mountain pony fell on the slope but, with preternatural agility, Bardel leapt free to bound downward as deer fled in all directions. Gethae fumbled for an arrow, but with a savage cry of battle Bardel fell on the neck of the single stag from above, caught it by backsweeping antler tines, wrenched it crashing to earth beneath him in a flurry of brush and bellowing.

Scrambling to avoid the razor hooves, whooping for the joy of it, Bardel strove to choke the stag into submission, and king and quarry tumbled into the dry creekbed. Something arced away, butterfly-bright in the sun, and Bardel's next whoop was of pained surprise. The stag found firm footing. Bardel, now impeded by a limp, was not so lucky. With a snort of terror the stag flew up the ravine and Boerab, bow drawn, feathers brushing his cheek, relaxed and saluted the animal with a smile. It had been too easy a shot.

While Boerab shared his smile with Gethae (for she had witnessed his act of mercy), others were hurrying to Bardel. It was Averae who found the great opal amulet adorning a shrub, its braided thong severed in the melee, and Dirrach who noted silently that possession was nine parts of the mana.

Bereft of his protection, Bardel had immediately sustained a gash below the knee. Bardel accepted the bleeding more easily than Boerab's rough jests about it; jokingly questioned the shaman's old wardspell; retied the gem at his throat; and resumed the hunt. But the king was sobered and his leg a bit stiff, and on their return to Tihan Bardel made good his wager. Boerab saw to the battle wound while Dirrach, pocketing an opal the size of a sparrow egg, retired to "rest" until evening.

*   *   *   *

Trembling with glee, Dirrach set the opal on a tabletop to catch the late sun in his chamber. He discovered the knot-loosening spell after sundown, and wasted time gloating while a warm breeze dried the last of the moisture from the hydrophane. Dirrach became glum as the spell seemed less effective with each repetition. The knock at his door startled him.

"Dasio the runner, sire," said a youth's voice. "I bring the girl Thyssa and her brother, Oroles. They said it was your wish," he finished tentatively. Unheard by the shaman, Dasio murmured to the girl: "If you should scream, many would hear. I've heard ill rumors of our shaman with—"

The door swept open to reveal a smoothly cordial Dirrach. With more expertise in sorcery, the shaman could have the girl at his whim; it was the brat who might hold the key to that darker desire for power. Affecting to ignore Thyssa: "I hope your mind is clearer tonight, boy, come in—but come alone."

Thyssa, stammering: "Our bargain, sire, I uh— might sweep and mend as payment while you examine the boy."

"Another time. The cub does not need distraction," Dirrach snapped, closing the heavy door. He bade Oroles sit, let the boy nibble raisins, listened to his prattle with patience he had learned from dealing with Bardel. He approached his topic in good time.

Oroles trusted in the shaman's power, but not in his smile. It became genuine, however, when Oroles admitted that the raven had pinpointed the thermal spring. "He brought proof," said Oroles. "It's at the head of a creek a few minutes west of Vesz. Is there a place called Vesz? Do ravens like raisins? This one wants better than fish guts. Do you have a pet, shaman?"

It was worse than talking with Bardel, thought Dirrach. "The village of Vesz is near our northeastern boundary, but several creeks feed the place."

"Not this one. It disappears into the ground again. The raven likes it because humans seem afraid to drink there. On cool mornings it smokes; is that why?" Oroles narrowed his eyes. "I think that's dumb. How could water burn?"

Dirrach rejoiced; he had seen warm water emit clouds of vapor. Three ridges west of Vesz, the boy went on, now straying from the subject, now returning to it. Dirrach realized that such a spot should be easy to locate on a chilly dawn.

Gradually, the shaman shaped his face into a scowl until the boy fell silent. "It's well-known that ravens lie," Dirrach said with scorn. "I am angry to find you taken in by such foolishness." He paused, gathered his bogus anger for effect. "There is no such spring or creek. Do not anger me further by ever mentioning it again. To anyone! Pah! You ought to be ashamed," he added.

Oroles shrank from the shaman's wrath as he withdrew a nutshell from his waistpouch. "Maybe there's no smoking water, but there's this," he insisted, employing the shell like a saltshaker.

"And where does the lying raven say he stole this?" Dirrach licked his lips as he spied, in the damp sprinkle of loam, a few tiny nodules of opalescence.

"Scraped from an embankment, fifty wingbeats south of the spring," said Oroles. "Sure is slippery dirt; my pouchstring keeps loosening."

Dirrach feigned disinterest, stressed the awful punishments that would surely await Oroles if he repeated such drivel to others. Dirrach could hear a murmur of male and female voices in the hall. "Your sister fears for your empty head, boy," Dirrach repeated as he opened the door. "Do not worry her again with your gift of speaking with animals." He ushered Oroles through, careful to show ostentatious concern for the boy, caressed the small shoulder as he presented Oroles to his sister.

And then Dirrach realized that the voices had been those of Boerab and the formidable Gethae, who strolled together toward the old warrior's chamber, tippling from a pitcher of wine. Both had paused to look at Dirrach in frank appraisal.

The shaman dismissed the youngsters, nodded to his peers, said nothing lest it sound like an explanation. Gethae only glanced at the spindly form of Oroles as he retreated, then back to Dirrach. One corner of her mouth twitched down. Her nod to Dirrach was sage, scornful, insinuating as she turned away.

Dirrach thought, *That's disgusting; he's only a lit-*

tle cub! But Gethae would have agreed. Dirrach returned to his chamber and his experiments, Bardel and his guest to theirs.

*　　*　　*　　*

The Shandorian runner was gone for two days, the Moessian for three; ample time for Dirrach to reassure himself that the fresh windfall of mana was genuine and resided, not in outlander sorcery, but in hydrophane opals. By tireless trial, error, and indifferent luck the shaman had enlarged his magical repertoire by one more spell. It would summon a single modest thunderbolt, though it was apt to strike where it chose, rather than where Dirrach chose. In that time he fought small fires, quailed at fog-wreathed specters, and ducked as various objects flew past him in his chamber. But as yet he had not been able to bring any of these phenomena under his control.

It was no trick to arrange a surface-mining expedition "on the king's business"—Bardel rarely bothered to ask of such things—and to stress secrecy in his instructions to the miners. Ostensibly the men sought a special grit which might be useful in pottery glaze. Dirrach was adamant that the stuff must be kept dry, for he had learned two more facts. The first was that the things were potent only when damp. The second was that only so much mana lay dormant in an opal. Once drained by conversion of its potential into magic, the stone might still achieve a dim luster; but it would no longer summon the most flatulent thunderclap or untie the loosest thong. The specimen won from Bardel was still, after many experiments, mildly potent; but the pinpoint motes in the loam sample were already drained of mana.

Dirrach saw his miners off from the trailhead above Tihan, giving them the exhausted grit as a sample. He regretted his need to stay in Tihan, but the outlanders required watching. The ten packass loads, he judged, would easily overmatch the mana of Bardel's great amulet.

"If you succeed, send a messenger ahead on your return," was Dirrach's last instruction before the packtrain lurched away toward a destination a day's hike to the north.

Dirrach turned back toward Tihan, imagining the paltry castle below him as he would have it a month hence, when he'd learned the spells. Stone battlements to beggar the ancient Achaeans; gold-tipped roofs; vast packass trains trundling to and fro; fearsome heraldic beasts of living stone, like those of legend, guarding his vast hoard of opals. And of course, a stockade full of wenches wrested as tribute from Moess, Shandor, Obuda,—it occurred to Dirrach that he was still thinking small. He must, obviously, conjure his great castle directly atop the thermal spring. It would stand on vapor, and soar into the clouds!

All the world would tremble under the omnipotent gaze of the great King Dirrach. Why not the great God Dirrach? Nothing would be impossible, if only he avoided some lethal experiment. A real wardspell was necessary, but so far he had not duplicated his accidental success with Bardel. A hot coal could still blister the shaman's finger; a pinprick could still pain him. Hurrying to the castle, Dirrach pondered ways to steal the great stone from Bardel's breast. He considered seeking out the cub, Oroles, to employ the raven as a spy—yet that would soon be unnecessary, he decided.

For Oroles, the raven was not the only spy. In Panon's smokehouse, the fisherman took a load of wood from the boy, chose a billet. "Don't ask *me* why all Tihan is edgy," he grunted. "Ask your friend, the ferret. Better still, don't. You'll have me believing in your gift, pipsqueak."

"I can't ask Thyssa," Oroles complained, " 'cause the shaman said not to. But everybody's so jumpy. . ."

Panon coughed, waved the lad out with him, brought a brace of cured fillets for good measure. "Huh; and why not? Green clouds form over the castle, fires smoulder on cobblestones near it, thunder rolls from nowhere,—some say the outlanders bring wizardry."

"What do you say, Panon?"

"I say, take these fillets home before the flies steal them from you," smiled the old man. "And steer clear of anything that smacks of sorcery." He did not specify Dirrach, but even Oroles could make that connection.

Panon's smile lingered as he watched the boy depart. If the old tales could be believed, neither Oroles nor Thyssa had much to fear from most magical events. Both had hearts so pure as to comprise a mild wardspell—even though Panon had often seen Thyssa embroidering her tales of the redoubtable Urkut; intoning foreign words of his, copying outlander gestures as her father had done to entertain her once. The girl had a marvelous memory for such things, but little interest in the occult. Besides, Panon mused, if such incantations worked, why was Thyssa not wealthy? Panon shrugged, winced, rubbed his shoulder. If his rheumatism was any guide, all Lyris would soon be enriched by summer rains.

*   *   *   *

Try as he might for the next two days, Dirrach could not entice Bardel into another wager, nor further physical risks. At length Averae exclaimed in the parley room, "I do believe Dirrach craves your amulet, sire, more than he wants a parley. Why not just give it to him and be done with it?" Dirrach maintained his composure while writhing inside.

"Because it's mine," laughed Bardel. "I even sleep with it."

Boerab exchanged a smile with Gethae and murmured, "To each his own."

"To each somebody else's," she rejoined, then cocked an eyebrow at the shaman; "however small."

Because Bardel joined in the general laughter, Dirrach imagined that he was being mocked by all present. The anxiety, frustration, and juggled plans of Dirrach kindled an anger that boiled to the surface; Dirrach leaped to his feet. The moist opal in his waistpouch validated his dignity as Dirrach unleashed his easiest spell with all the gestural strength he could summon, cloaked in verbiage. "Let those who think themselves superior be loosened from conceit," he stormed.

The next instant, all but the invulnerable Bardel were grasping at clothing as every knot within five paces was loosened.

Oil lamps fell from lashings to bounce from floor and table. Boerab and the outlanders fought to hold their clothing—and Dirrach himself was depantsed.

Without a word, eyes flashing with contempt, Gethae gathered her clothing and strode out, living proof that she could combine nudity with pride. Averae sputtered and fumed, his gaunt rib cage heaving with pent rage as he struggled to regain his finery.

As for Boerab, the staunch warrior faced Dirrach over the head of their openmouthed king, leather corselet and gorget at Boerab's feet. "Mana or mummery, Dirrach," he roared, "that was a stupid mistake! You've affronted guests; friends!"

Dirrach retied his trousers, fumbled with waistpouch, a furious blush on his features. "The first offense was theirs," he said huskily. "High time you learned a little respect."

"I'll show respect for lumps on your head," Boerab replied, taking a step forward. "Stop me if you can."

"Hold, Boerab," cried the king, finally on his feet. "What will our guests think?"

"They'll think we need to strangle that piss-witted child molester," said Boerab. But Dirrach had already fled into the hall.

"Who is king here, you or I?" Dimly, Bardel recognized the need for a regal bearing; for a measured response to this sudden turn. "For all you know, Dirrach could turn you into a toad, Boerab."

Averae, who had watched the confrontation in silence, now spoke. "Well spoken, sire. It strikes me that you may have need for more than one shaman. A balance of powers, as it were."

"But we don't have—" Bardel began, and stopped.

"You have only Dirrach," Averae said for him and added gently, "We know that, Bardel; but mutual loathing and mistrust are brittle bases for a treaty. With Dirrach, I fear—I fear I'm giving counsel where none is asked," he finished quickly.

"No, go ahead and say it," Boerab urged. "Everybody knows our fine shaman is a sodomizer of children."

"Everybody but me," said Bardel, aghast.

"And who was to tell you?" Boerab spread his big hands, then launched into a description of what he and Gethae had witnessed outside Dirrach's chamber. As usual, the tale grew in the telling.

Averae was not surprised. "Dirrach is unwelcome in Moess because he preyed sexually on the young," he said without embellishment.

In the hallway, Dirrach ground his teeth as he listened, enraged at the irony of it. The king was still ignorant of his real transgressions, but seemed ready to punish him for imagined ones!

"Have Dirrach confined in his chamber," said the king sadly, "until I can decide what must be done. If you *can* confine him," he added with sudden awareness.

"Cold iron is rumored to block any spell," Averae said mildly.

"And I have an idea where we can locate another who's adept, or could become so, at Dirrach's specialty. I don't think I really thought it possible until now—the mumbo-jumbo, I mean," Boerab said.

Dirrach heard heavy footfalls, thought of the cast-iron ax, and ducked into a shadowed alcove as Boerab huffed past. The shaman could not return to his chamber now—but perhaps he would not need to.

At dusk, Dirrach emerged from hiding. By turning his tunic inside out and jamming sandals into his belt, the shaman passed unrecognized in the dusty byways of Tihan. Twice he melded with shadows as men clattered by, clumsy with bronze weapons they seldom used. Dirrach felt certain he could command their fear, or at any rate their trousers, in a confrontation. Yet the uproar would locate him. Thunderbolts might not help. Dirrach made his way unseen to a hayrick near the palisades, climbed atop it, and sniffed a breeze chill with humidity as he burrowed into the hay for the night. He willed the rains to hurry; they kept most folk indoors.

Summoned in early morning, Thyssa ran with her friend Dasio before a damp wind as Dirrach, in his perch at palisade height, scanned northern hills for sight of a messenger of his own. While the girl made a fetching obeisance to Bardel, wondering what her sin might be, Dirrach spotted his man astride a pack-ass. Shouldering a stolen mattock, blinking dust from his eyes, Dirrach trudged out from the untended palisade gate into the teeth of the wind to intercept his man.

In the castle, Thyssa was tongue-tied with astonishment. "I, sire? Bubbut, *I?*" Her pretty mouth was dry as she stared up at her king. "But shamans are men, and I know nothing of necromancy or—*I*, sire?"

"Oh, stand up, Thyssa, he's not angry—are you, Bardel?" Boerab dug a gentle elbow into Bardel's ribs. No, not angry, Boerab judged; but perhaps a bit bewitched. How like the dunderhead to notice beauty only when it lay beneath his nose!

"I'm told you might be of great service to Lyris,"
Bardel began, "if you can but recall your father's ancient spells. Dirrach has crimes to answer for. The
question is, could you replace him?"

Slowly, Thyssa was persuaded that this was no
trick to convict her of forbidden arts, and no royal
jest. She admitted the possibility that Urkut, in his
tale-spinning, might have casually divulged knowledge of occult powers which he had learned in distant lands. Urkut's failure to make full use of such
knowledge might be ascribed to disinterest, fear of its
misuse, or even to a blocking spell. Added Boerab,
who did most of the coaxing: "Now it's time to find
out, Thyssa. How well do you recall Urkut's tales,
and what secrets might they hold?"

Thyssa nodded, then closed her eyes in long rever-
ie. It seemed an age before a smile of reminiscence
tugged at her lips. Hesitant at first, Thyssa knelt before cold ashes in the fireplace. A few gestures
mimed placement of invisible kindling, whirling a
nonexistent firestick, other actions not so trans-
parently pantomimic—and then the barest wisp of
smoke sought the flue. With practice, she coaxed a
flame upward, but turned in fear toward Bardel who
bent near, his huge sweat-stained amulet swinging
like a pendulum.

Too dull-witted to consider the dangers, Bardel
grinned at her and winked: "Now try it on the
flagstones."

Flagstones burned, too. The problem was in
quenching them. Thyssa finally thought to reverse
her gestures and after some failures, sighed as the
flame winked out. Thyssa was, of course, wholly in-

nocent of the oral shorthand equivalents which
sorcerers of old had used. Thyssa wondered aloud
why Urkut had never put such spells to work around
the cottage, then recalled another of her father's anec-
dotes. She got it right on the third try. Boerab made
her erase the spell, laughing nervously as an oak
table levitated toward the roof. Again, the reversal
worked when she did everything in order; the heavy
table wafted down.

Urkut's spell over food was not to be deduced as a
preservation spell just yet. Thyssa tried it on their
noon meal of bread, beer and fruit, but nothing obvious happened and the experiment was soon con-
sumed. Thyssa had no inkling, yet, that their lunch
could have been stored for a century without losing
its freshness.

His belly full, Bardel urged the girl to devise some
spell of a more warlike nature. "The sort of thing that
gave warlocks their name," he said. "We may need it;
don't forget, Dirrach is at large."

Boerab shuddered. "And if it goes awry? Thyssa
toys with thunder as it is."

"The nearest my father got to a curse, so far as I
know, was when he'd speak of shamans and their
powers," she reflected. "Then he'd say a prayer for
deliverance—and do something like this." She began
a two-handed ritual; paused with a frown, reversed
it; began anew with a nod of satisfaction.

The trapspell, far older than any of them could
know, was very special. Lacking mana to energize it,
Urkut had never known—until too late—whether it
worked. Fundamentally it was a shrinkspell, positive-
ly polarized against evil and those who employed it

by magical means. Only those present—the king, the girl, the warrior, and a mouse near the hearth—could be the beneficiaries, and then only in proximity to a source of mana. As with the preservation spell, nothing spectacular happened; but the room grew oppressively warm.

"I guess I forgot something," Thyssa sighed.

Boerab, rising: "You're the best judge of that. But perhaps you'd best stop for now. Think back, and make haste slowly; as for me, I'll just make haste. There's bad weather brewing and we'll never find Dirrach in a storm."

"I hope it cools things off," Bardel nodded; "even my amulet is hot."

Thyssa took her leave, welcoming warm rain on her face as she hurried homeward. It did not seem like the kind of weather that would cool Tihan much.

*   *   *   *

Dirrach's messenger bore the best possible news, and estimated that the grit-laden packass train was no more than a half-hour behind. The man had no way of knowing Dirrach's outlaw status and dutifully returned, on the shaman's orders, to direct the packtrain toward a new destination. Jubilant, Dirrach took shelter from intermittent wind-driven showers under a stand of beeches. From his promontory, he could see groups of Tihaners searching lofts and hayricks. It would be necessary to commandeer an outlying farmhouse and to detain the miners until he had puzzled out ways to make himself invincible.

And how long might that take? Perhaps he should retreat further into the hills with his mana-rich ore. Later he could return with gargoyles, griffons, even armies of homunculi. . .

As the little group of miners struggled from their protected declivity into the open, heading for their new rendezvous, Dirrach allowed himself a wolfish grin. Then his features altered into something less predatory as he watched the packtrain's advance.

The skins over the packs gleamed wetly, and the lead miner fought a cloud of biting flies—or something—so dense that Dirrach could see it from afar. Then pack lashings parted—untied themselves, Dirrach surmised—and both skins began to flap in the wind. The lead packass took fright, bucked, stampeded the animals behind it, and in the space of three heartbeats the procession erupted into utter mind-numbing chaos.

* FLASH *   BLAMMmm . . .

A great light turned the world blue-white for an instant, thunder following so close that it seemed simultaneous. Now the miners waved, sought to slow the maddened animals, and fled through clouds of grit as the pack contents whirled downwind, spilled into the air by the leaping beasts.

One miner disappeared in a twinkling. A packass, then another, flew kicking and hawing in the general direction of Tihan—but at treetop level, a sight so unnerving that miners scattered in terror. Paralyzed with impotent rage, Dirrach knew that a trickle of water into one of the packs had triggered a series of events; a series that had scarcely begun.

As the storm waxed, Dirrach hurried toward one pack animal in an attempt to save some of its load without getting downwind of it. Dirrach had seen a man vanish in the stuff, but could not know the man had reappeared safely under his bed in Tihan. The packass saw Dirrach, rolled its eyes, grew fangs the length of shortswords, roared a carnivore's challenge. Dirrach scrabbled into a tree with a bleat of stark horror. From his perch, he could see clouds of fine grit blowing over palisades into Tihan in a monumental manaspill.

*   *   *   *

Old Panon blinked as a grit-laden gust of wind whirled past him at the dock; steadied himself above his nets with outflung arms. He could never recall later what he muttered, but the next moment he stood amid a welter of fish, all flopping determinedly from the lake into his pile of net. Panon sat down hard.

On merchant's row, the bronzeworker followed a reluctant customer outside in heated exchange over prices. A blast of wind peppered them both and suddenly, his heel striking something metallic, the customer sprawled backward onto a pathway no longer muddy. It was literally paved for several paces with a tightly interlocked mass of spearheads, plowpoints, adzes, trays; and all of gleaming iron.

The tanner was wishing aloud for better materials when he ducked out of the foul weather to his shop. He found his way blocked by piles of fragrant hides.

The produce merchant spied a farmer outside, rushed out to complain of watered milk, and braved a gritty breeze. The men traded shouted curses before discovering that they stood ankle-deep in a cowflop carpet. It spread down the path as they fled, and more of it was raining down.

An aging militiaman paused in his search for Dirrach to surprise his young wife, and found that he had also surprised one of the castle staff. The younger man cleared a windowsill, but could not evade the maledictions that floated after him. He hopped on through the gathering storm, his transformation only partial, for the moment a man-sized phallus with prominent ears. He elicited little envy or pity, since most of Tihan's folk had problems of their own.

Bardel was informed by a wide-eyed Dasio who could still run, though for the time being he could *not* make his feet touch the ground, that the end of the world had arrived. The king howled for Boerab, aghast as more citizens crowded into the castle toward the only authority they knew.

One extortionate shopkeeper, perched on the shoulder of his haggard wife, had become a tiny gnome. The castle cook could still be recognized from his vast girth, but from the neck up he seemed an enormous rat. Bardel saw what the citizens were tracking into the castle, wrinkled his nose, and stood fast. "BOERABBBB!"

The old soldier stumped in, double-time, sword at ready, but soon realized he was not facing insurrection. "It pains me to say this," he shouted over the hubbub, "but Thyssa may have made some small miscalculation—"

"All this, the doings of one girl?" Bardel's wave took in the assembled throng.

It was Dirrach's erstwhile messenger, breathless from running, who set them right. "No, my lords," he croaked. "The shaman! I saw it begin with my own eyes." Convinced as always of Dirrach's powers, the man attached no value to the windborne grit. Thus he did not describe it, and a great truth passed un-noticed.

"Shaman. . .Dirrach. . .the molester," several voices agreed, as Boerab and his king exchanged grim nods.

Bardel motioned the eyewitness forward, hardly noticing that the knee-high shopkeeper was already beginning to grow to his original size. "Tell us what you know of Dirrach," said the king, "and someone fetch the girl, Thyssa."

*   *   *   *

Sodden and mud-splattered, Dirrach made his way unchallenged in waning light to the unoccupied cottage of Thyssa. He moved with special care, avoid-ing accidental gestures, forewarned by personal ex-perience that the hydrophane fallout was heavier in some places than in others. He no longer entertained the least doubt that Bardel enjoyed magical protec-tion so long as he wore the amulet.

Face-to-face intrigue was no longer possible, and Dirrach judged that raw power was his best option. It should not be difficult to wrest the small stone from Oroles. Far greater risk would lie in finding the means to steal the king's great opal. Perhaps an in-visibility spell; Dirrach had seen the passage of some unseen citizen as footprints appeared in one of Tihan's muddy paths. The shaman had seen Bardel lose his amulet once through accident, knew that it could be lost again through stealth.

Dirrach plotted furiously, filing vengeful ideas as he ravaged the small cottage in search of the waist-pouch of little Oroles. He knew it likely that the boy had it with him, but trashing the place was therapeutic for Dirrach.

If the locus of power lay in hydrophanes, then none but Dirrach himself could be allowed to have them during the coming power struggle. Once Bardel was dead—and stiff-necked Boerab as well, by whatever means possible—the shaman could easily fill the power vacuum he had created. Time enough then to organize a better mining foray!

Dirrach paused at the sound of approaching footfalls, strained to pull himself up by naked rafters, and stood near the eaves in black shadow. One of the voices was a youthful male; Dirrach held his one-piece bronze dagger ready.

"I'll be safe here," said Thyssa, just outside.

"So you say," replied Dasio, "but I'd feel better if you let me stay. Why d'you think the outlanders packed up and left so fast, Thyssa? As the Shandorian woman said, 'only fools fight mana.' Who knows what curse Dirrach will call down on Lyris next?"

Stepping into view below Dirrach, the girl shook her head. "I can't believe he intended all this, Dasio." There was something new in Thyssa's tone as she closed the door; something of calm, and of maturity.

Dirrach heard footsteps diminish outside, grinned to himself. He had no way of knowing why this peasant girl's self-confidence had grown so, and did not care. One of the rafters creaked as the shaman swung down.

Thyssa whirled to find Dirrach standing between her and the door. "Where is the cub? No, don't scream," the shaman ordered, the dagger his authority.

"Cleaning a huge pile of fish with a friend," she

said. "Perhaps Panon should thank you for them, Dirrach. And don't worry, I won't scream. It may be that you and I have some things in common."

At that moment, Oroles burst into the cottage. Dirrach grasped the lad, enraged both by the surprise and the girl's treatment of him as an equal. Oroles squalled once before Dirrach's hand covered his mouth. Sheathing his dagger quickly, Dirrach wrenched the lad's waistpouch away and cuffed Oroles unconscious. Then Thyssa did cry out.

The shaman was not certain he could silence her quickly and made a snap decision. "The cub is hostage to your silence," he snarled, slinging the boy over one shoulder.

Thyssa's hands came up, churning a silent litany in the air. "I don't think so," she said, and Dirrach found himself rising helplessly into the eaves again. He dropped the boy who fell on bedding, then locked one arm over a rafter as Thyssa reached into a corner. She brought out a wickedly tined fish spear.

Thyssa, advancing, clearly reluctant with the spear: "Even a rabbit will protect her young."

Dirrach saw that the tines of bone were bound to the spearshaft with sinew, invoked his simplest spell with one hand, and barked a laugh as the sharp tines fell from their binding. But something else happened, too; something that startled Thyssa more than the loss of her weapon. She stepped back, hugged the boy to her, gazed up at Dirrach in fresh awe.

Dirrach felt distinctly odd, as if the rafter had swollen in his embrace. "Get me down," he hissed in hollow braggadocio, "or I turn you both to stone!"

Thyssa reversed the levitation spell, naive in her

fear of his power—though that fear was fast being replaced by suspicion. The shaman released the rafter as he felt the return of his weight—or some of it, at least. He sprawled on the packed earth, then leaped to his feet and stared up at the girl.

Up? He glanced at himself. His clothing, his dagger, all were to the proper scale for Dirrach; but he and his equipment were all a third their former size. Thyssa's trapspell, dormant until now, had energized in response to his evil intent with magic.

The shaman's fall had been a long one for such a small fellow and, in his fury, Dirrach summoned a thunderbolt. The flash and the sonic roll were dependable.

And so was the trapspell. Thyssa covered her ears for a moment, blinking down at a twice-diminished Dirrach. His dagger was now no larger than a grassblade and fear stayed his steps. Obviously the girl had done this; what if she stepped on him while he was only a hand's length tall?

Little Oroles stirred, and Thyssa kissed the boy's brow. She was shaken but: "I was wrong, shaman," she said evenly. "We have nothing in common."

Her eyes held no more fear, but Dirrach thought he saw pity there. This was too much to bear; and anyway, he already had the boy's manastone. Dirrach snarled his frustration, squeezed through a crack in the heavy wall thatch, hurled himself out into the night.

*　　*　　*　　*

Had the trapspell depended on windblown particles of opalescent grit, Dirrach might have grown tall within the hour. But Thyssa's spell had drawn on the mana of Bardel's amulet, and the shaman had a long skulk to the castle.

His mind, and other things, raced with him before the keening of a fitful wind. He listened for telltale human sounds, found that he could easily hide now, kept his small bronze fang in his fist. Dirrach recalled the vines that climbed past the royal chamber and knew that stealth was a simple matter for one of his size. Now and then he paused to listen. It seemed that even the leaves teased him as they scurried by.

At last he reached the castle wall, planning headlong. Once he had cut his way through the upper-story thatch, he could hide in the king's own bedchamber and wait for the king to sleep. And Bardel slept like the dead. A predator of Dirrach's size and cunning could easily sever the amulet cord, steal the protecting manastone, then slice through a king's royal gullet. After that, he promised himself; after that, old Boerab. It was a shame that Averae had already fled, but a grisly vengeance could be brewed later for that one; for the girl; for all of them.

He sheathed his tiny dagger, tested a rope of ivy, and began to climb. Then he froze, heart thumping as he perceived the eyes that watched him with clinical interest; eyes that, he realized with shock, had been on him for some time. . .

*   *   *   *

Three days after the storm, a healing sun had gently baked away the last vestige of moisture in the dust of Tihan. Citizens tested their old oaths again and found that it was once more possible to enjoy an arm-waving argument without absurd risks.

After a week, Bardel called off the search for his

elusive shaman, half-convinced that Thyssa had imagined Dirrach's shrinkage and half-amused at the idea of danger from such an attenuated knave. But he did allow Boerab to post dogs around the castle, just in case.

Boerab's ardor to collar the shaman went beyond duty, for Gethae of Shandor had been spicy tonic for a veteran campaigner, and blame for her leave-taking could be laid squarely upon Dirrach. The garrison joke was that Boerab had exchanged one lust for another.

Thyssa refused to leave her cottage. "I'm comfortable there, sire," she explained, "and Oroles would soon be spoiled by palace life. Besides, my, ah, friends might be too shy to visit me here." She turned toward Boerab. "Intercede for me, old friend!"

Boerab slapped an oak-hard thigh and laughed. "Fend for yourself, girl! Just threaten to levitate your king. Or turn him to stone; you're capable of it by now, aren't you?"

"No," Thyssa admitted sheepishly. "And I don't seem to be inspired unless I'm in my king's presence. But I'll spend some time practicing here daily, if that is your wish."

Bardel kicked at a flagstone. "Why not, uh, spend some time with me just for amusement? I have eyes, Thyssa. Your friends aren't *all* bashful; only Dasio. And all your other friends are new ones. What does that tell you?"

"Just as you are, Bardel," Thyssa replied, "and what does *that* tell me?"

"Damnation! What does my runner have that I don't?"

After a moment: "Long familiarity—and shyness," she said softly. She exchanged a glance with Boerab and did not add, *and wit.*

Bardel pulled at his chin, sighed. "I've offered you everything I can, Thyssa. My larder and my staff are at your orders. What more can we do to seal your allegiance?"

She smiled. "But Lyris has always had that. One day I'll move to the castle, after Oroles has grown and—" she paused. "Oh, yes; there is something you can do. You might have those dogs taken away."

Boerab: "They won't harm you."

"It's not for my sake. Oroles has a friend who lives around the castle. The dogs disturb it greatly."

Bardel's smile was inquisitive: "*Around* the castle?"

"A ferret, sire," she said, blushing. "Oroles no longer claims to talk with animals, except for one. Don't ask me how, but he's convinced me that he really can do it. You have no idea how much he learns that way."

The men exchanged chuckles. "Let's wait for news of Dirrach," Boerab said, "and then I'll remove—"

"Oh, that's another thing," said Thyssa. "Oroles tells me the ferret spied a tiny manlet the other night, and it described Dirrach perfectly. It watched our shaman do the strangest things.

"Oroles told the ferret that it was lucky Dirrach hadn't seen it; that the shaman was a bad man."

"Quite right," said Boerab. "I'll double the dogs."

"I'm not finished," Thyssa went on. "The ferret replied that, on the contrary, it found Dirrach a lot of fun. In its own words: delicious."

A very, very long silence. Boerab, hoarsely: "I'll remove the dogs."

Bardel: "I wonder if you could make ferrets become very large, Thyssa. You know: guard duty, in Lyris's defense."

Thyssa: "I wonder if you would want them thus. They are not tame."

"Um; good point," said the king. "Seems a shame, though. If you can talk with them, looks like you could tame them."

"Only that one," Thyssa shrugged, and bade them farewell in time to meet Dasio for a stroll.

The secret of the hydrophanes was intact. Not even the ferret knew that one of Dirrach's opals remained, permanently damp, in a corner of the animal's belly.

Tihan's folk were to learn caution again during rainy weather, though with each hapless employment the mana was further leached from the glittering motes in Tihan's soil and roof thatches. Meanwhile, Lyrians began to gain repute for a certain politeness, and greater distance from their king. It occurred to no one that politeness, like other inventions, is a child of necessity.

As a consequence of the manaspill, even the doughty Boerab agreed that mana was a hazardous reality which few cared to explore. If a king's presence was fecund with mana, then perhaps royalty bore divine rights. Europe's long experiment had begun.

"... but fear itself."

Steven Barnes

The door opened slowly, a slender wedge of light falling, widening, on the porch. A withered hand fumbled at the latch, finally holding the screen door open so that a small, sinewy shadow could enter.

"There you are, T'Cori," Judith said, bending stiffly to scoop the tortoiseshell kitten into her arms. "Momma was afraid you weren't coming back tonight. That might have been very bad." She scratched its ear, listening to the bubbling sounds it made. T'Cori backed her head against Judith affectionately. "No, Momma needs you tonight."

Judith peered out into the street, her dark sunken eyes unblinking as they searched for movement. She shook her head slowly and closed the door, mouth drawn into a taut line.

She set T'Cori down by a saucer of milk in the kitchen, then walked slowly back into the living room, lowering herself into her sewing chair, a vast, flowery thing that nearly swallowed her whole. One thin hand pressed against her chest and she closed her eyes, listening to the labored workings of an ancient and worn machine. "No," she whispered sternly. "No. Not yet. Not tonight." For an instant, there was shooting pain along her arm and she inhaled deeply, sucking air in slow, desperate gulps, opening her eyes again as the pain receded. "Tomorrow," she said, the color coming back to her face. "Tomorrow. Tonight is mine."

There was a knock on the door, three raps, then two. A smile wound its way onto her face and she pushed herself out of the chair, paused to adjust a black-rimmed portrait of a dark smiling man which sat upright on the mantel.

"He's come, Josh," she said to the picture. "He's a good boy." Tears burned at her eyes; she fought them and won.

Again, the knock on the door. Judith walked to the front door and opened it again, swinging the screen door wide for the gangling young man who stood in the dim glow of the porch light.

"Good evening, Aunt Judith," he said, stepping into the room. He pecked her on the cheek and she returned it, scowling.

"You growing a beard, boy?" She closed the door and waved him to an overstuffed chair across from her sewing chair. A single white candle burned on the table.

He nodded and handed her a small brown bag. "Tryin' to. Here. Just some milk and eggs, but the freezer looked a little empty last time I was over."

Judith clucked happily as she took the bag into the kitchen. "Bless you, Ronald."

The young man crossed one denimed leg over the other and stretched back in his chair until he heard grinding sounds in his neck. T'Cori popped into his lap and he wiggled a finger behind her ear as he looked around the room he knew so well. In nearly every spare inch of space, there were plants. Potted ferns, sweet potatoes floating in water, long-stemmed roses cut weeks ago and in some miraculous way

still a symphony of bright reds and yellows. Creepers wound about thin doweling set high in the wall, and a miniature citrus tree bore grafted branches of oranges, limes and lemons, surviving with only window light and love for nourishment. There was more, much more, but he refused to waste time cataloguing, instead breathing deeply of the sweet, sharp perfumes that filled the air.

Judith shuffled in from the kitchen, a plate of oatmeal raisin cookies balanced in one hand, a glass of milk in the other. Ronald filled his grin with sweetness and wet, and sighed contentedly.

"Uncle Josh would be proud of you," she said, her gaze unwavering as she studied him. She lowered herself back in her chair. "A college man now. Where do the years go? It seems like last week when you came up to the front door and asked if we had any bottles you could haul."

"Mmmfh," he said, then paused to swallow. "I can still remember his answer, too: 'Don't ever ask folks to give you nothin, boy. You ain't gonna make no money like *that*. You got to give 'um a piece of yourself.' And he took that old corncob monster out of his mouth, dragged me into the back yard, and taught me how to hoe." He laughed, high with old memories. "You people were always mighty good to me. I couldn't love you more if you had actually been kin." He seemed embarrassed, and attacked another lumpy brown pastry ferociously.

"He . . . We loved you, too." He tried to tell himself that he was imagining things, but there was something . . . unnerving about the way her eyes were set. Something unfamiliarly restrained about her voice. "You learned fast. You knew how to work, boy, and how to listen. Even when Josh was just . . . tellin' stories."

The tension left him. "My God . . ." a sudden disapproving stare, ". . . uh, my gosh, how could I help but listen? All that about Pirander and Ibandi and the magic that used to be in the ground. You wait. In between botany classes I'm going to find an excuse to do a paper on African folk myths, and blow *everybody* away."

Judith looked at him for a long, painful moment, then spoke. "Perhaps you will. Perhaps not."

He paused in mid-mouthful. "Why not? They were

great stories."

The last cookie was eaten, and she waited until he had drained his glass. She sat, watching him silently until he began to shift in his seat. "There was one last story, Ronald. One that Josh always wanted to tell you."

Broad muscular shoulders hunched in confusion. "Why didn't he? I'm a little old for stories now."

"No." Her voice crackled in the room, more force in it than he had ever heard, and he found himself recoiling.

"Aunt Judith? Are you . . ." He started from his chair.

She waved him back, angry with herself, now. "I'm sorry, boy, It's just—there is one last story, and you must hear it." The room's shadows deepened the wrinkles in her face until it seemed like a piece of dark, dried fruit.

"Well . . ." He slumped back into his seat until its softness engulfed his body. "Sure." He found his smile again. "This is your time, Judith. All you said was that you wanted to see me before I left for college. I came running. Lay it on me."

She stood slowly, gathering her thoughts. "Josh told you about the magic, the *mana*, and how greedy, foolish men used it up with their spells and ceremonies. Pirander brought the news of the vanishing power to his homeland, and to his twin brother Ibandi."

"Right. I remember now. Pirander took his followers to Australia. They became the Abos, right?"

"Correct." She smiled. "But we never did tell you what became of Pirander's brother, Ibandi. He was also a mighty wizard, one more farsighted than his brother. If *mana* was going to run out, then it was of no use to move to more and more remote lands. Eventually it would be gone from everywhere, forever. Ignoring that fact was merely abandoning future generations."

She pulled an ancient world globe from a darkened corner of the room, and spun it until she reached Africa, then traced a finger down until she reached Johannesburg, then just a hair southwest. "This is where they lived, Ibandi and his followers, and where they stayed. The one change was that they began using the remaining magic to amass knowledge, knowledge that would be used in a final, desperate attempt to find a source of *mana* that would never dry up, that might serve them for generations yet undreamed of."

A wrinkle of curiosity touched Ronald's face. "And did they succeed . . .?"

*   *   *   *

You will lead. That was what the dream had said to him, as clearly as a clean wind whipping through the grass. *You will lead.* Nagai fought to keep his excitement from bubbling past the wall of control. He squatted on his string-tight haunches, hands resting easily on his thighs.

He watched the Dinga priest speak to Pulolu, the elder Father of the Ibandi. Every ten days the priest came, his sagging belly painted with runes, and his head festooned with gaudily dyed feathers. Nagai didn't like the man, although, or perhaps because, he always smiled, and sometimes laughed with a booming voice. The Mothers and Fathers had always told him that the Dinga were their friends, that in exchange for a little food, the Dinga protected them

from enemies. That the Ibandi owed the Dinga much.

Nagai waved a fly away from his offering, watched the priest posture. Why would they need the protection of the Dinga? Was not all the Body in accord? Something about it made him feel sour in the stomach. The girl ahead of him in the line stood, bearing her armload of tubers. The Dinga priest smiled, the sharp tips of his teeth brushing fleshy lips.

Nagai stood, felt a droplet of perspiration trickle down his back, and calmed himself. He forced a neutral expression to his face and strode forward. The boy halted, bare toes gripping dirt and tiny pebbles as he extended his bowl of fruit. "A gift to our friends," he said automatically.

The priest patted his head with a great moist hand, and Nagai chewed at his lower lip. The fat man picked up one of the yellow ovals and buried his teeth in it, his eyes widening in pleasure as the juice welled up over and dribbled down a stubbled cheek.

Another pat on the head. Nagai smelled the sourness of the other's body. *Fear. This man is afraid.* But that was absurd. If they were of the Body there would be nothing . . .

"You Ibandi," the fat priest said, laughing, eyes tiny and wet. "How do you call up such magic from this soil? Do the plants listen to you?"

Nagai smiled.

The priest chuckled again, and passed the basket to the Dinga warrior who stood behind him. The man stacked the basket into the cart waiting, now almost filled with the week's offerings.

The Ibandi lad ran from the gate as soon as his burden was lifted, and made for the nearest stand of

fruit trees. Reaching them, he stopped and looked back at the front gate and slow-moving line of contributors to the Dinga cart. Most were older than his sixteen years: Nagai had only been allowed to make offering for the past four months.

It was part of the process of becoming a Father. Or, for that matter, a Mother. Slowly, he was being eased out of his childhood, taking on a few more responsibilities, gradually learning what it was to be a Coordinator.

But what was he feeling from the Dinga? He didn't understand, not at all. The cart was finally filled, and began to move out of the gate, pulled by four men. Always the same men. Always staring straight ahead, silent, unblinking.

Once, the first month of Nagai's contributions, he had come close to one of the four men, standing in front of him and watching as a fly crawled across the doughy face, across an open eye without a blink. Ashan, his father, had taken Nagai by the hand and led him away quickly, refusing to answer questions.

Still the Coordinators, both Mothers and Fathers, refused to talk about it. "You will learn," was the most response that ever came, before the inevitable smile and "why don't you go play now?"

The boy watched as the gate closed behind the Dinga priest and his cart, and the Coordinators walked back into the central village with drawn, worried faces.

A child ran up to one of them, and there was an automatic warm smile and hug; the ugly moment had passed. Nagai stretched, breathing deeply to cleanse lungs and mind. Immediately he felt the gentle knowledge tickling at him like a feather, and the joy came bubbling up out of his worry like fresh cold water. "I come, sister."

Nagai ran from the grove into the central village compound, taking a moment to spin from the path of three running children. One of them, a dark, sweet-faced child who giggled "Nagai!" turned on her heel and stopped. "You're going to be a Father today." She grinned challengingly.

He shook his head at her. "Everybody knows more than me."

"That's why you're going to be a Father. You don't know enough to be a kid anymore." He swatted at her playfully and she took off, chasing after her friends, now disappearing around a hut.

He tried to find a speck of irritation to hurl after her, and came up empty. She was right. He couldn't feel the *mana* as once he could. As any child in the village could. But he knew things now. He knew more of the world outside the high fence. He knew of the Dinga, and their fear. And soon, he would be a Father, a Coordinator. And he would guide the children, as he had been guided from earliest memory, *coordinating* their feelings into the fields and streams. Keeping the Ibandi centered in the Body. And as a part of the Body, they were fed by the forests, the streams, the fruit of the earth.

These were the earliest truths he could remember. *Life is your birthright. As an organ of the Body, you need fear nothing but fear itself.* Fear was corruption and death. Fear was cramping muscles and a clouded mind. Fear was anger, and hatred, and all things evil.

And the Dinga priest had smelled of it.

The old woman at the front flap of the birthing hut

147

nodded toothlessly as she stepped aside, "It is time."

Daytime vanished as the flap swung down. Within, the only light was the glow of a tiny brazier.

The birthing hut was large enough for twenty at a time, and it was filled. Except for Nagai, no male Ibandi older than five years was in the room. Seven children sat in a ring surrounded by twelve ancient Ibandi women who sat, legs folded and eyes closed, humming softly. The children giggled as if they were being tickled, the liquid sounds of their pleasure weaving into a melody that complemented the humming of the older women.

In the center of the circle of moaning women was Nagai's mother, Wamala. Her legs were crossed, her hands rested easily on her knees. Her moist plump face was peaceful. The dim light in her womb grew brighter.

She chanted softly:

"Ibandi, lord of the Ibandi, bring forth thy new daughter bloodlessly, in peace and purity. Ibandi, lord of the Ibandi, grant her thy strength. Ibandi, lord of the Ibandi—"

The women in the hut chanted and sang, perspiration running in their age-furrowed faces. Musk-sweet incense hazed the air blue.

Wamala's body shuddered, each tremor rippling outward from the glow beneath her navel. Her eyes focused on her son, and her chin bobbed in acknowledgement. The light in her belly grew brighter still, and extended past her skin to shimmer in her lap. The chanting of the elders grew more intense, and the light began to congeal.

At first, just the suggestion of an infant's form shifted within the light, then huge dark eyes formed,

pinpoints of sparkle within the greater glow. Gradually shadow filled in detail, and arms, legs and trunk emerged. The haze faded and the infant, air still shimmering about it, blinked slowly with translucent lids.

Mylé, the senior midwife of the Ibandi, stood heavily. Twisted with years, she moved as if her joints were filled with sand. "Ibandi be praised, a girl child." She stalked across the hut like a black crab, only her face animated. "Come," she took Nagai's hand in a brittle grip. "You're a man now, boy."

Silent, he let her lead him to the center of the circle. Nagai dropped to one knee before his mother.

"Nagai."

He touched her outstretched hand to his cheek. "Mother." The tiny glowing thing in her lap gurgled. Its aura expanded until it filled the hut, washing a jeweled spectrum over the skins and woven mats that covered the walls.

Nagai drooped his shoulders, and searched within himself for the fluttering tingle that would focus his sister's *mana.*

From a loose cloud, the cascade of light condensed into tendrils, snaking and darting in the air all about her. She bubbled with delight.

"She is pure magic," he murmured.

"As are all children," Wamala said. "As were you, once." She was tired, and the strain of the ritual rasped in her voice. But her eyes were alive as they scanned the taut planes and gentle contours of his body. "You have seen the bloodless birth now. You have not been allowed to witness it in eleven years."

His sister tried to wrap him in her light, but it fuzzed to mist under her control. "I had almost forgotten. Almost."

"Now is your time for learning," Wamala breathed, her eyes fighting to close. "You are ready for Fatherhood now. Go—your sister will comfort me. Go. There is much to be learned and done."

He touched his lips to her forehead, and then even more gently to the head of his sister. "When she is named, I would like to be present."

"Perhaps. We will see what the Mothers say. Go now. Go to the Fathers." Her voice weakened, and he knew that it was time for him to leave. One of the midwives lifted Wamala slightly, sliding a layer of moisture-absorbent matting beneath her.

"Leave now," Mylé whispered. "She must release the birth water, and it is not for you to see."

He stood and bowed. "Mother," he said, treasuring the word, knowing that it would never again have the same meaning between them. "Good-bye." Her eyes closed, glazing, and he backed out of the hut and left.

Some of the children waited outside the birthing hut. Many were nude, small black bodies glistening with the afternoon heat. Others wore clothing as their bodies began to ripen with age: those with younger brothers and sisters would soon be eligible as Coordinators. Those without . . . he saw among them the familiar face of Bolu, his hair woven like a child's, incongruous above the corded body. But everyone of the tribe knew that Bolu's mother would never have another child. Bolu would remain hers, caring for her until the day she died. Only then would he ever be permitted beyond the Gate. Only then might he seek Fatherhood.

Nagai sang to them wordlessly, touching their hands as he walked back to the front gate. He touched their minds and felt them laugh, feeding him *mana*. It seemed as if each of them were giving him a single thread, a single silver strand that he wove into a cocoon about himself. And there, in his womb of energy, he could feel things he had forgotten, and truly knew himself as part of the Body. But now he just played with it joyfully, knowing that today was the true beginning of his life.

At the front gate he didn't have to explain or ask, it was opened for him, that he might go and find his father, Ashan. He was not turned away at the Gate, or told to find a Father to guide and protect him. He was of age, and now had a sister. He might well be a Coordinator, a Father, by the end of the day.

He ran past the outer fields where grains and tubers were coaxed from the earth, hopping over irrigation ditches and seedlings as he sped. What would it be like? The world of the Coordinator's mind. The Mothers used the children for bloodless birth, for healing, for growing food. The Fathers used them for hunting, fishing and luring.

He heard the rush of the stream, and knew that Ashan would be somewhere near. Nagai brushed the reeds aside and started to yell.

Something fierce and wet clinched his ankle. Nagai hopped back, shaking his foot violently, stifling a yelp of surprise. He kicked free and scrambled back three paces before stopping to see what it was.

The arm had thick, grayish skin, its elbow clumsily articulated. Higher up towards the shoulders it was spotted with tufts of hair that ran up into the scalp, where they joined a ragged shock of dark brown mane.

Its eyes flared greenly up at the boy, and short

sharp teeth clacked feebly together.

Even as Nagai watched, the fire died, and the thing's body relaxed with finality. Nagai jumped as a broad hand clapped on his shoulder.

"You did not feel me, and you did not feel the Ghoul. You are indeed a Man now."

Nagai's eyes darted from the alien corpse to his father. Ashan's face was unlined, except for three rows of parallel scars that ran vertically on each cheek. His hair was dusted with gray, but the extreme erectness of his carriage made Time an abstraction.

"A Ghoul?" The puzzlement in his voice was genuine.

"It should never have come so near to the village." His father's expression was difficult to read, something stirring behind the placid brown mask that confused Nagai terribly. "It is an enemy of our— friends—the Dinga."

"But father . . ." Nagai found his attention returning time and again to the body of the Ghoul. Its muscles were growing flaccid. "Why didn't the Dinga keep it away? Why have I never seen one before?" The Ghoul was half-covered in water. Already, scavengers were investigating the possibilities.

"The Ghouls are a were-people, and came to our land in search of—sustenance."

"Why didn't our friends keep it away if it is dangerous?"

"The Ghouls are powerful."

"More powerful than our friends?"

His father seemed to wince at the word. "Very nearly. The Dinga won the war, but it has drained them. They have used much *mana*." Ashan nudged the sodden Ghoul with the tip of his sandal. The corpse twitched, then was still.

"Why did they come here?"

"Mana," Ashan said.

"But . . . why *here? Mana* is everywhere."

His father sighed, and sat the boy down on the grass. "There are many things that you do not yet understand. One is that not all people use the life-force as we do. Some use it to move objects, or change metals, or create life. This takes great concentrations of *mana*, nowadays only to be found in rare areas, like ours. We, the Ibandi, use it only to harmonize ourselves with Nature, to teach us of the Body. Only in the bloodless birth do we violate natural order, that we might bring our children into the world knowing nothing of pain or fear. There is *mana* in children, great power, but they begin to lose it as they learn fear. They are cut off from the flow of Nature."

"And the Ghouls? The Dinga?"

Ashan shook his head proudly. "No. This is our secret. They work their crude magics, draining power from the earth, or—" he looked sharply at his son who sat, fascinated, "—from the bodies of men. And their eyes are blind to the gentle *mana* that flows to us from stars and sun and moon. Too subtle for such as the Dinga to understand or use. A pattern connecting all living things into the Body."

He stretched out his hand and pointed to the lush greens and browns of the plain they lived on, to the mountains far to the north. "Once, a piece of star struck this plain, and spread its power throughout. It is for this that the Ghouls fought the Dinga."

Nagai couldn't take his eyes from the Ghoul. Dead, without a mark on its body. Already it was losing color. Starved for *mana?*

Ashan sounded thoughtful. "Perhaps I should wait for the Fathers to tell you these things, but you need to understand as much as you can, if you are to . . ."

Nagai had heard that silence before. It was an impassable void that told him that his father had already said too much.

Ashan stood, pulling his son to his feet. They walked to a spot near the nets, where another Father Coordinated four small, laughing children. The air about them shimmered as with heat.

The *feel* of their *mana* was in the air. He knew that he could guide them, Coordinate them. He felt the hunger growing, the empty feeling in his stomach. He wanted to reach out, to join with them and call fish to the nets, to repel insects and diseases from the crops . . .

"Soon, you will be a man. Already, I know you feel the waning of the strength you knew as a child." Ashan's eyes were sharp and alive as he drew near. "You will continue to lose *mana* and gain knowledge —if you become a Father this day."

"I am ready."

"Are you?" His father extended his hand. "Flow with me."

Father and son extended palms until they were within a hair of contact. Fingers upright, the hands danced together, only the barest layer of air separating them. Ashan fluttered his fingers, and Nagai responded fluidly, again, the fractional distance maintained. Small, then larger circles and patterns. Never separating more than a hair's breadth, never touching. Finally, the lean, corded arm of the older man dropped to his side. Ashan nodded approval. "You have learned."

"I am ready."

"The first challenge is ready for you—has been ready for days." He clasped his son's shoulder. "Once, centuries ago—" His face grew strained, and again Nagai felt the oddness. "Before the Dinga came, my father's father many times removed was the king of our people."

"But we have no kings . . ." Nagai sputtered, remembering the dream. "We need no kings. Our friends . . ."

"Yes," Ashan said bitterly. "Our friends, the Dinga." He leaned close, until Nagai could scent the sharpness of his breath. "But perhaps one day we will need kings again. And perhaps we will not need friends. You must be prepared."

Although unanswered questions swam in his head like nervous fish, Nagai nodded his confidence. "I am ready."

"Then go. The first test awaits."

*   *   *   *

The sick feeling returned to the pit of Nagai's stomach. If there had been food there, he would have found a waste ditch to empty it into. But his stomach had been empty for two days, since Wamala had first entered her birthing cycle.

He squatted, clearing his mind, minding his breathing, feeling his weight sink into the ground. The more he relaxed the more it tingled. Not the same as he had as a child, though; then, it had seemed that the world was a crisscrossing spiderweb of energy that flowed from all directions, gossamer threads that could be woven by the skill of a Coordinator.

Once, his father had shown him a piece of rock, glassy gray and pitted deeply on the surface. There was so much *mana* in it that it burned him to be near it. He had vomited immediately, while Ashan beamed with pride.

But now, consciousness of the strands was a dim, elusive thing, found only in the deepest states of relaxed wakefulness. He yearned to be a Coordinator.

Olo grinned at him from the other side of the Amphitheater. There was a diagonal chunk of tooth missing low on the left side and Nagai laughed back at him. He remembered the game of tag that had ended with his own arm skinned from wrist to elbow, and Olo's mouth bloodied against a rock. Olo had won.

Younger and leaner than Nagai, Olo was not yet so knowledgeable, but his vision was clearer . . . .

There were no children in the Amphitheater, only the gathered Mothers and Fathers, sitting quietly on the ground in concentric rings. Wamala sat across the ring from Ashan, with the Mothers. She was pale, and sat wrapped in blankets, but would not be dissuaded: she had come to see her son.

There was one other within the ring: Weena. Her hair had been braided finely, in tight rows and swirls, proclaiming her preparedness for Motherhood.

Nagai tried not to think of her, to think only of the contest to come. Was it truly only three months since the three of them had run, playing as children play, through the streets and groves? Only three months since the Fathers had prepared her for Motherhood. She had ceased playing with the children after that night, and had begun her wait for the first eligible

Father.

Today. It would be either Nagai or Olo.

Through half-lowered lids Nagai measured the sweet curves of her naked body, and the strength of her eyes. Even at this distance he felt her, and knew that he had to have her.

Olo stood, Nagai unfolding from his crouch in the same moment.

Slowly, as if a drum were beating in a distant corner of the village, their feet began to move in unison, tamping down the hard-packed dirt of the Amphitheater.

They approached each other, and Nagai felt Olo's *mana* and knew his opponent, younger, to be the more powerful. But this was not a contest of strength, and Nagai was unconcerned.

The two of them were close now, and both turned sideways, their shoulders almost grazing before each slipped to a side and slid by the other without touching.

A sound began, deep in their throats. It echoed their breathing, deep and organic to the movement. Not singing, not speaking, but something that blended with the rhythms of feet and swaying bodies until it became impossible to say which throat made what sound.

Nagai swirled and capered, the contortions of his waist squeezing the air from his chest, the backward arcs expanding his lungs again. For an instant he grew dizzy, then he found the balance between himself and Olo, and the two of them moved in the Body as sound filled the Amphitheater.

At last there was a disturbance above them, a fluttering of wings, and both dancers paused, their torsos

halting in mid-twist. On each, the light oil of exertion reflected the afternoon's waning light, highlighting the tautly-muscled planes and valleys of their bodies.

Nagai stood with his arms splayed out to the sides, directly behind him the frozen figure of Olo. Nagai could feel his rival's heat, smell his sweat. His stomach burned, and he slowed his breathing to a crawl, relaxing, relaxing . . .

The fluttering grew closer, but still neither looked up. Once there was a quick flash of a tiny white figure, then nothing but fluttering.

Olo trembled a bit, then relaxed. Nagai felt it, and visualized as he did when a child: Spiderwebs. Silken strands of life. One to the other. Living things, sacred things. All interlocked by the strands. Every living thing . . .

Sound, very close, of settling wings, then the weight of a small body on his shoulder. Nagai turned his head, smiling to the tiny white bird that sat there, cocking its head as if mystified with its own actions.

A sigh of release, echoed by the Coordinators, and Olo stepped away from Nagai. As he left the Amphitheater, he was biting his lower lip savagely. There would be blood.

Nagai stood alone, facing Weena. She rose to her feet in a floating spiral and glided to him, searching his face and body with her eyes.

She was perhaps two inches shorter than he, and stood very straight, her body covered only with a tiny woven breech cloth. When she became a Mother, she would cover her breasts as well, but not until then.

Their eyes met, and he felt himself being drawn to her, as if he could lose himself in the depths of swirling brown. He stayed very still.

She took his hand. "Come." Again, the Coordinators sighed.

The second trial was conducted in a small unadorned hut behind the groves, near the fence. Weena walked ahead of him. He felt lightheaded, and tried to center his thoughts. What would this be . . .?

She brushed aside the bead curtain and beckoned him inside. Brushing past her nearly burned his skin. They sat across from each other in the darkening room and savored the tension. The moistness and heat, the sweet sight and smell of her made him feel giddy.

"I lost my Childhood three moons ago." Weena said simply. "But I must have a mate to become a Mother."

"As must I to become a Father." Again Nagai thought of Olo's bitten lip. "Olo will wait until the next moon, and again contest. I hope he attains . . ." Nagai smiled mischievously. "But I am glad that he will not attain with you."

Only the barest flicker of her expression showed joy. "Olo will win Fatherhood one day. Today, we must deal with what is. I am a woman, and with you, could be Mother. If you pass your third trial, I can make you Father. Will you open yourself to me? Will you let me know you, that I might choose?"

Perspiration had blossomed on her cheeks, tiny beads slighter than dewdrops. Her expression was still, only the rise and fall of her shoulders, the gentle swell of full young breasts, spoke of life.

He had to trust. This was not the Weena he had played games and skinned knees with. The nights she had spent with the Fathers had changed her. His body knew the difference, and it tightened his stomach to dwell on it.

"Yes," he said finally. A trickle of sweat worked its way out of his armpit to slide down his side.

She reached out and touched his thigh just above the knee. Her fingertips warmed him.

Touch me, she said without speaking. Not in words, not in images but with the sudden creation of a *void.* He stretched out to touch, conscious of her hand sliding gradually up his thigh, the heat increasing until it became almost, but not quite, unpleasant.

Their eyes met across a space of a few inches, and they breathed each other's breath and formed the Body as they sat, crosslegged. She felt the tenseness of his body, the locked muscles and emotional scars that made him retreat from her.

She spoke softly as she touched him. "We are born in perfection. As we learn fear we lose vision, we lose suppleness, we lose contact with the Body. This is a consequence of understanding, of growing older. Fear is the destroyer. Only Love can give us back our perfection, for a few precious moments we are pure beings again, in the Oneness of the Body. If I join with you I will take your fear and pain, and let you see what once you saw as an infant. For that instant, you will have both knowledge and understanding, and you will become a Coordinator, reborn and renewed."

Nagai felt the tension leaving his body with the gentleness of her touch, and he could *see,* could feel the *mana* about him as he hadn't felt it for more years than he cared to remember. He felt it warm and cleanse him, clinging without pressure and guiding without judgment. The heat within him flared, the light clouding his vision.

She drew back. "No. Not until the third trial." Her voice was heavy and slurred, with a heaviness that balanced the lightness he felt in his own body. He wanted to beg her to continue, but sensed that it would be wrong.

For long moments she seemed burdened, then she straightened her back and exhaled sharply. Her smile relieved him.

"Yes." she said softly. "We need each other. You and I can understand each other." She sighed deeply. "Here is the next piece of knowledge that you need, Nagai. All things, especially living things, are like the mushroom. Mushrooms live in clumps, but are apparently separate entities. Only looking to their roots can one see that such a clump, with a dozen flowerings, is actually one creature.

"So are we all. All things that exist are forms of the same thing, only Pain and Fear prevent us from seeing the roots, or the invisible seeds that spread life. We perceive things as being different—in sizes, colors, locations and times. These are but the flowerings. The roots are in the Body.

"We understand this as children, as infants, as small clumps of life in the womb. Pain and Fear prevent the energy of life from flowing freely through us, and we lose what once we understood, replacing Understanding with its shadow, Knowledge.

"Nagai, we are the only ones who know that children brought into the world without violence, in an atmosphere rich in love and *mana* are open, and free, and can feel the connective energies. They are protected from the world, that they might stay within the Body totally, for in becoming a Coordinator you gain perspective, and lose the natural acceptance of things.

"Love gives it back to us. When we lie together, you and I, I will take you into my body and you will take me into yours. I will show you things that you have long forgotten, and give you peace."

"And I will see . . ." He left the question hanging. Nagai felt his limbs tremble with anticipation.

"What I see. You need me, and I need you. Together, we will make a child. You, and I, and our child will make up one small Oneness in the Body."

She stood, bending to trace her finger along his jawline. "Do not try to understand. You cannot. It must be shown." Her tone dropped, and she lowered her eyes shyly. "We belong to each other now, Nagai. For Always." They touched, and Nagai wanted only to stay with her, to learn the secrets hidden behind the warm brown eyes.

Torchlight flickered and popped in the Amphitheater. Only the Fathers were there. Their faces were heavily lined with stains, and together, in perfect harmony, they swayed to and fro in the gloom.

Nagai stood before them, silent, as the Eldest stepped slowly to the center of the Amphitheater. Age had eaten Polulo's face into a ruined hollow. He walked in a rhythm of threes; foot, foot and the probing tip of a gnarled cane.

"Young Nagai, you seek Fatherhood. A woman has chosen you, so your final test lies with us—" his voice was a hissing sound. "The Fathers."

"I am ready."

"So you believe. If you would win the scars of Fatherhood, you must show that you can Coordinate the *mana.*

Nagai repeated the ritual words that his father had prepared him to say. "I have shown this, with the first test.

"You must show that you are ready to be absorbed into the Body."

Nagai stood tall, tasting the power and the victory that would soon be his. "I have shown this also, by the second test."

The old man shook his head. "It may be better for you to refuse your Fatherhood, young one."

Nagai's hands clenched in shock. This was not part of the ceremony! He searched the faces of the men ringing the fire, and learned nothing. Even Ashan's face seemed a stranger's.

"N-no," he stammered. "I am ready."

Pululu clucked, deep in his throat. "We pray you are."

"Give me my task," he said firmly, reassured to hear his voice ringing clear and strong.

"Your task is to bring the children of the village—every one of them—here to the Amphitheater. Here, you will join with them, Coordinate them—and slay the Dinga."

The sound of the last words rang in Nagai's ears, burning like drops of flaming oil. His tongue seemed clumsily thick. "But-but why? They are our friends—they protect us—"

"From themselves, Nagai. You were spared the truth, as are all the children. Today you learn."

There was a murmur of agreement from the assembled Fathers.

"Three hundred years ago the Dinga came to our land, seeking the power in the earth. They are a wicked people, who had renewed their own powers by ritual murder when the *mana* grew short. Only the cleverness of our forefathers spared us a bloody fate, for they were more powerful than we. But they could not grow food as we grow it, or fish or hunt as we. So we have supplied them with food, half of our crops and catches, in exchange for peace to live our lives."

Nagai tried to find words that expressed the empty confusion in his gut. "But we—we can continue, can we not? Surely we need not spill blood." Thoughts tumbled from mind to mouth in a torrent. "And—and if they are more powerful than we, how can I destroy them?"

"The were-people," Pulolu said with certainty. "They changed everything here. They warred with the Dinga for months."

The young man's mouth hung open numbly. "I never knew."

"We have paid a heavy price to insulate you from such knowledge, such pain. Your task now is to repay what we have given you. The Dinga defeated the were-people, but now their strongest wizards lie in exhaustion. The *mana* in the ground is gone. Tomorrow, or the day after, they will hunger, and they will look to the closest source of life-energy at hand—the Ibandi. This time, fruits and fishes will not dissuade them. This time," and his voice was a cold and unyielding wind. "We must strike first."

Nagai was silent. Reds and blacks crowded the edges of his sight, and he smelled his own fear.

Fear the destroyer, his mind echoed, and he shut it down desperately. "Time. I need time to think."

"No!" Pulolu shrieked now, corded throat stretching as he lifted his face to Nagai. "It must be done now! Now! Tonight! Or we lose everything!"

"But—"

"No arguments. Accept or decline, that is all."

Nagai felt his legs buckling, and smelled a now-familiar aroma from the men of the circle, something that he had never smelled from them before. Sour. Heavy.

They can fear. Cooordinators can fear. The ground seemed to drop from beneath his feet. Knowledge did not protect from Fear. Vision continued to deteriorate . . .

In that moment he understood—*he was the most powerful member of the Ibandi.* For that day, that moment, no other Ibandi had as much Vision and Knowledge simultaneously.

Only he could do it. Only he could save the Ibandi. Their eyes stretched out to him in hunger. *You will lead.*

There could be only one answer, but his voice still cracked.

"I accept."

*   *   *   *

The children of the Ibandi were eighty in number, and they sat, child by dark child, in concentric rings, dotting the Amphitheater.

Even to the very young ones, they sat in total silence, bodies still and waiting. No sleepiness, no wandering of attention, although the sun had disappeared beneath the horizon five hours earlier. Even Nagai's sister was among them, cradled in the arms of Olo. Bolu the man-child was there, quiet, waitful, an infant's eyes peering out of his stubbled face.

Nagai crouched in the center of the rings, balanced on the balls of his feet.

The children fed him *mana*. He felt the lines appear, invisibly thin things that connected one infant to another, to child, to adolescent. The lines radiating from the youngest children were hottest, purest. Nagai gathered them with his mind. Forgotten totally was the great mass of the Coordinators who stood back from the circle. Watching. Hoping.

He spun and tightened with his mind until the strands became visible light, ropy luminescent bands that crisscrossed about them until it became a net, then a solid cocoon of light that surrounded the children in a glowing hemisphere.

One with the Body, he imaged with every deepening breath. Until the flesh seemed to melt from his bones, and a cool cleansing wind whistled in his mind. And he soared, seeing . . .

The torches and lights of the Dinga flickered, casting wraiths of darkness on the walls of their adobe homes. The fat cattle mulling in the pens sniffed the air, and even the guards pacing the edge of the city hunched their shoulders and peered into the darkness.

There is a void here . . .

Men and women of the Dinga turned in their beds. A few awoke and strained with tired ears for sounds that never came.

There is sickness here . . .

The Dinga priest awoke, staring blindly into the darkness. His tongue slid dryly over the points of his teeth, and he roused himself to a sitting position. There was nothing to be heard in his small, bare room, and no light to see. He knelt up from the thin mat he slept on, and groped out for his robe.

Come, creatures of the earth, creatures of the air.

There is death, and wickedness, and disease here. It is a corruption of the Body.

The temples of the Dinga were silent and still, except for one, where a single robed priest genuflected, then prostrated himself before a swollen-bellied idol. A brazier nearby cast a dull glow, scenting of burnt herbs and blood.

And from the forests they came. From the ground. From the skies.

There is corruption here. On the morrow it rises to slay.

A single scream split the Night, and a naked figure dashed from a hut and rolled in the street, clawing at face and body. Tiny biting things, stinging things, scrabbled on his skin, and the man writhed in the gutter, groans of pain and fear babbling in his throat.

He was not alone. From every corner of the city there came cries, screams as all of the vermin that dwelled in chimney and larder and sewer, all of the flying things that should have slept in bunches within paper nests, and the terrible red ants that bit so fiercely and relentlessly, poured into the homes and onto the bodies of the Dinga people.

In the temple, the priest staggered, slamming into curtains and tables, screaming as he staggered toward the altar. He clawed at his eyes, but the crushed bodies of dozens of their kin did nothing to dissuade the winged demons that plucked and darted.

He stumbled into the brazier, knocking it to the ground and falling atop it. His body jerked spastically.

At last he twitched more gently, as the screams and sobs of the Dinga died away into the night, and finally there was silence.

*   *   *   *

The sounds of screaming were lifted in the wind, carried to the Ibandi. They stood, the Coordinators, Mothers and Fathers, outside the dome of light Nagai had spun on the Amphitheater grounds. When the whispering screams faded away, no man or woman there could mistake the message in the silence.

The stars glared pinpoint-bright and cold. The light from the cocoon cast twisted, dim shadows.

Only the sound of tense breathing, and the distant cough of a wild dog filled the still air of the village.

Then the hemisphere began to waver, and it appeared that tiny balls of light were peeling back from the surface. The hole formed looked like a wound ripped in living flesh.

Nagai stood there, staring at them, through them. There was no anger in his voice, or even accusation. The words were almost toneless, but for a massive fatigue lingering beneath the surface that threatened to bow him.

"You didn't tell me. You never told me—" his eyes would not focus, even when he looked directly at Pulolu. His throat quivered. "They hurt so much—the Body believed me and destroyed the diseased flesh, but their *pain*, their *fear!*"

A hint of pleading crept in now, and his body sagged before he caught himself. "How could you? Why didn't you tell me how much it would *hurt?*"

Wamala took an uncertain step toward him, but she stopped short as if she had run into a glass wall.

"Nagai—you don't need to fear me—"

He looked at her curiously, trying to remember something lost in a jumble of pain.

"Mother? Why . . ?"

She whined, trying to speak. Fingernails splintered against the air, and she dug at the ground with her feet. "Give me my baby," she sobbed finally, "Give me your sister."

Slowly, painfully slowly, he shook his head. "No. All of you must live with the knowledge of what you did, as must I. The children must never know." He clutched himself, trembling with the effort to remain erect. "Oh, mother, it burns—" He caught himself again, and his eyes focused at last. "I'm taking them. I'm taking them where you won't find them, and when they're safe, I will die."

"But the children!" Pulolu hobbled forward, mouth working numbly. "You have not the knowledge. If you take them, they will never learn enough—"

"That may be true," Nagai hissed, "but they will still be more than you." At last he took a backwards step, his chest heaving with effort. "None of you—none of you interrupt me, or try to stop me, or you will die."

He retreated into the ruptured hemisphere. It healed behind him sluggishly.

*　　*　　*　　*

Pulolu turned to the others, searing them with his gaze. "We cannot allow this thing," he said weakly. "The children cannot . . . cannot survive without us."

"What can we do?" The question arose spontaneously from a dozen throats.

The Eldest looked to the stars, the bright, cold clusters of light that dominated the night sky. "It is Nagai who has proven weak. For the good of the Ibandi, he must die."

"No!" Wamala screamed. Ashan stood beside her,

gripping her shoulders as she twisted.

"You cannot kill my son." Ashan said. "His is the Power now. None match him in strength."

Pulolu peered up at Ashan, stared until Nagai's father turned away from the ancient, pitted face. "Are you of the Body?" Pulolu edged closer, until Ashan gave ground. "Do you speak for the Body, which lives forever, or for Ashan, a bit of flesh which will one day putrefy?"

"I speak . . ." A great sigh went out of him, like water out of a ruptured skin. "For the Body, of course . . ." Ashan felt Wamala's body tense in his arms. "But—but who could do this thing? He refused to even let his mother touch him."

"Yes . . . but he had already broken ties with her. There is another, who had just begun to live her bond. Yes, another . . ."

He scanned the group until he found Weena. Small, bright-eyed Weena, shrinking back from him into an unyielding wall of human flesh.

"No . . ."

There was silence again, save for the shuffling footsteps of old Pulolu. He reached out a clawed hand to touch her face. "Would you have your people die? Would you doom the children?"

"I wouldn't . . . but I couldn't hurt Nagai." She fumbled for words. "We are joined—"

"He is no longer Nagai!" Pulolu screamed, his voice rising to a painfully high pitch. "He has allowed his weakness to eat away at him. He was an inadequate vessel for his power."

Weena tried to run, but strong arms held her fast.

"Would you let the Ibandi die? Would you kill the children, and us, and yourself, that one imperfect organ of the Body might live? Would you thus damn yourself?"

There were tears in her eyes, but they only welled hugely, did not spill, until she shook her head slowly, miserably. Until she heard Pulolu's grunt of satisfaction.

*   *   *   *

Weena had been washed and anointed. Her skirtlet was dyed in flower patterns, and her cheeks were painted in wedding glyphs. She stood holding a basket of fruits and yellow vegetables, just outside the shimmering barrier. Her small, exquisitely lovely face was expressionless, and there was no trace of emotion in the voice that softly called.

"I am here, Nagai. I am yours. I will enter your world, or I will die. The choice is yours." She waited long anxious heartbeats, then took a short step forward, then another, until her balance committed her to the final step, and she crossed the barrier. At first there was searing heat, and light so bright it turned closed eyelids into sheets of flame. Then she was through.

It was cold within, and very dark. Each exhalation fogged and hung in the air like pale butterflies. She waited for her eyes to adjust.

At last she could see a few small, still figures—the children of the Ibandi. They lay splayed about as if in exhaustion, limbs and torsos overlapping in a giant sprawl. They made no movement or sound.

In the middle of them, cross-legged and staring at her emptily, sat Nagai.

He seemed not to be breathing at all, merely sitting, waiting, his face the face of a dead man. His mouth hung slack.

Weena stepped over the unmoving form of an infant, one part of her mind trying to ignore the way it was curled up on one side like a tiny corpse. The other part tried to identify it. Whose child was that? Whose puffy-cheeked baby? It lay in dreamless sleep. Protected from knowledge, from pain and fear by the ashen figure of Nagai.

His eyes were red and wide. She stepped over a final child and held her basket of fruit out to him. Her body was racked with chills.

Slowly, as if the impulses crawled along his nerves like spiders climbing webs, he pulled his mouth closed.

His voice was a faint rattle. "Why . . ." he said, then yawned torpidly. "Why have you come?"

"I came—"

One hand worked its way up out of his lap, a single finger raised. Her words jammed in her throat like chunks of splintered bone.

"No lies," he hissed.

The urge to turn and run was a physical thing, tugging at her like snare lines. She felt the cold penetrating her body, numbing the marrow.

"It is not safe for you, here," Nagai said, each word heaved out with a sigh.

"I came . . . because I am yours. You are mine. We are pledged."

For all the change in his visage, she might have been squawking or squealing instead of speaking words.

Then . . . something crept into his eyes that she had never seen in him, or any other being. A longing or need beyond the need for food or shelter or even breath. A deathly fatigued desperation. "I wish . . ."

175

Then he dropped his head to the ground. "No, you must leave."

She knelt before him, setting her bowl down, and brought her face very close to his. "We belong to each other."

"No . . ." he said, trying to find the strength to turn away.

The muscles in her arms trembled as she came closer, lifting his chin to gaze at him.

She felt his need. Smelled it, sweet and sour in her mind. It rang in her ears like the rushing blood of a burst heart. Like a torrent rushing to fill the void she came to him, and all thoughts were swept away.

Still he fought, for an instant more he fought to control himself, then something shattered. Tears spilled from his eyes and he reached for her hungrily, felt her warmth melting the ice that filled his belly, felt himself drifting, soaring . . .

*   *   *   *

Weena awoke first. She twisted away from Nagai's sleeping body and clutched a hand to her stomach, sobbing in the darkness.

Nagai's peaceful expression made the pain recede for a moment, then she remembered why she was there. Weena reached into the basket, under the cool firm shapes, and pulled the knife. She curled her fingers around it carefully. An iron blade, wound with fiber at the hilt, five inches of edge and point nestled in her fist.

Gasping now, she got one hand braced on Nagai's shoulder and levered him over onto his back. Voices screamed in her ears, fingers of dead hands crawled up the lining of her stomach.

Fear like this never dies, unless ...

For the last time, she bent over and kissed him on the throat, on the warm hollow so recently discovered. He slept on, peacefully.

Then she raised her hand, screaming her pain and sorrow, and drove the knife with all her strength up under the ribs and into her heart.

*   *   *   *

Nagai awakened slowly, listening for the voices, feeling for the cold, or the crawling fingers, but there was nothing. Without turning, he knew what he would see.

Weena lay curled on her side, her face calm now. Her hands still grasped the knife buried under her ribs. He brushed her cheek, walking its roundness to the long curve of her neck.

The Children were waking. They rubbed their eyes with tiny fists, and yawned. Olo touched Weena, uncomprehending but unafraid. He stood, and picked up one of the babies.

Nagai gathered up their *mana* and exhaled a thin, even stream. The dome about them began to glitter, then glow. It burst into sparks and dissolved.

The Mothers and Fathers stood outside the shielded area, clustered, silent, staring.

No movement, no challenge. Nagai felt nothing for them. The strands, the slender strands that had bound him to the Ibandi were broken, lost forever.

Without a word, the children formed into a ragged line, the largest carrying the smallest. All heads were directed toward Nagai, at the head of the line.

Mothers sang to their infants, Fathers threatened and promised, but all eyes remained on Nagai. No parent could cross the thin, shimmering barrier that

surrounded the line.

Pulolu spiderwalked to the front of the line, his mouth working silently. "You dare not!" he screamed at Nagai. "What you do is sacrilege!"

Nagai's gaze was focused on the horizon and beyond. Without glancing down at the Eldest he said: "Sacrilege? And what of the task you set me to?"

The old man flinched back, "It was for you! It was for the children."

"You lie," Nagai whispered. "It was for your fear."

"They will be separated from the Body."

"Your fear has already done that. There is no route to the Body through you."

"Many will die . . ."

"We all die. To go is to die. To stay with you, in this place, is worse."

Without another word, they walked from the village of the Ibandi, toward the mountains to the north. None tried to stop them. Nagai passed his mother and father on the way out. Wamala swallowed and looked away from him, but his father nodded shallowly, almost imperceptibly, and Nagai found the trace of a smile to give them.

"Nagai!" Pulolu screamed, waving his stick. "May you rot in the sun! Ibandi damn you for what you do here! May your belly crawl with worms—"

The line moved on, out of the gate and the village, out of sight of the Ibandi forever.

*　　　*　　　*　　　*

Judith stopped talking and swallowed hard. Ronald was sunk back in his chair and gazed at her over the top of the candle that now burned low in its holder.

Finally, he cleared his throat. "And what happened then?," he asked uneasily, "What happened to the children?"

"They suffered. Some died of exposure, some starved. Some merely sickened." She retreated back from the candle flame until her face was lost in shadow, and her voice sounded like a thing from the dead, distant past. "Nagai and the older children coped as well as they could. Some of them were adopted by other tribes. Some fell prey to slavers. . . ." The words drained away. Her eyes were reflecting pools within the shadow, and he could see that her hands were knotted and tensed until they seemed to fuse with the chair arms.

Ronald felt something cool brush the back of his neck, and warmed it with his hand. He smiled warily. "Well . . . that's really something." A broader laugh, now. He tried vainly to pierce the darkness that shrouded the reflecting pools. "It's sure a lot different from the other stories . . . ." He half-rose from the chair, glancing at the door, to his wristwatch, to her unblinking eyes. "I guess I oughta be going now—"

"No. It is not a story. It is true." Her voice was a whisper that carried clearer than a shout, and there was a terrible, acid, churning in his stomach. "It is true. The story has passed from husband to wife, from mistress to man, for more years than I can guess." Now she leaned out of the shadow, and the light made her face seem all grooved shadow and burning eyes. "And the knowledge—what is left of it, has passed, too—"

Ronald felt the breath rasping in his throat and stood, horrified.

"It's true, Ronald, it's true." Her voice was begging now, the words tumbling out like children's blocks.

"And there is only one obligation—to pass it on. I received it from Josh. I told him that I couldn't do it, couldn't pass the gift to a man I wasn't married to. He never pressured me. He knew . . . ."

She stood facing him, her body shaking. "But my time is coming, I can feel it now. And I know that it would be wrong to die without passing on what is left of the gift. The Vision."

He raised his hands to his ears to block out her sound, drowning, terrified of the old woman who stood before him, craving something he could never give. "No! This is a lie." Suddenly there was understanding in his face, and he lowered his hands. "God, Judith. Oh, Lord, I should have known. Living here alone . . . I know how attached you were to Uncle Josh." He spoke quietly, pityingly. "I can find someone for you to talk to—"

She shook her head sadly, and reached into a side pocket, pulling out a seed, a single, small, yellow seed. "I knew you could not believe. Neither did I, at first. I must show you what I can."

T'Cori sat on the table, licking her paw, and didn't flinch as Judith took her in a withered hand. The kitten curled there, purring.

Judith milked her cheeks several times, then spat into her right palm, onto the seed. Then she closed her eyes and relaxed, humming almost imperceptibly.

T'Cori's purr deepened, and it looked up at him, eyes half-lidded. Its head grew heavy and it snuggled down into her left palm with a sighing growl.

For a few seconds there was nothing. No sound, no movement. So still was Judith's body that Ronald wondered . . .

Then the seed, in the small pool of clear fluid, began to split. A slender tendril of stalk worked its way out as he watched, and a gossamer network of root pushed free from the opposite side. In the space of two minutes it reached a length of five inches, absorbing the liquid in her palm until it lay there, dry and impossible, a tiny plant barely five minutes old.

The room whirled around him. She opened her eyes. There was no madness there, no lust, no danger. It seemed that they were windows to another time, a time when miracles were commonplace, and where Ronald had never walked except in dreams.

"You . . ." he licked his lips with the dry tip of his tongue. "You can teach me this?"

She shook her head. "No. I *must* teach you. Please, Ronald. There is no one else to give it to."

He leaned on the top of his chair, feeling his youth and strength, seeing the life stretching before him like an open road. And suddenly he saw her, truly saw her, not as an aging, weathered body, but as a spirit cloaked in human flesh, a spirit joined to a heritage stretching back to prehistory. A spirit begging him to help keep that heritage alive.

"What . . . what must I do?" he said at last, his voice unrecognizable.

She nodded, and gently deposited T'Cori on the table, and with the same hand cupped the candle flame. A whiff of breath and it wavered sharply, then died.

She faced him across the gulf of darkness and years, and held her hand out to him. Ronald looked at it uncertainly, then watched his own reach out to take it. Her hand was firm, and dry. And warm.

184

Strength

Poul Anderson and Mildred Downey Broxon

Night still held the western horizon when Shalindra found the dead sea-unicorn. It stretched sleek amid kelp, timbers, and storm-drowned birds. The sorceress knelt in the wet sand. Zaerrui had mentioned that once, in his travels a hundred years ago, he had seen a cup carved from such a horn. A king drank from it to ward off poison.

One of the beast's great brown eyes stared skyward at the wheeling gulls. Soon they would land and feast. Shalindra stroked the flank—cold in death, but not fish-slimy. What must it be like when alive?

Behind the ragged peaks of the Heewhirlas the sky glowed pale. This early, Shalindra walked the beach alone, but soon the townspeople, too, would be out searching for gale-brought treasure.

Doubtless any of them would offer her the horn but doubtless, also, he would exact a price: most likely a healing spell. Those were failing everywhere. She must hoard her magic, in hope of making her son Llangru strong, or at least controlling the tremor in his hands so he could learn to write.

She sighed and looked down at the huge dead beast. The spiral horn measured a good cubit longer than Shalindra stood tall. She pulled. It held fast.

She needed a saw sharp enough to cut bone. There was probably one back at the library, but to find it would take time. Meanwhile someone else might claim her prize. Best not to squander power on a warding spell; best, instead, to hurry.

In her haste, stumbling over the littered beach, she almost fell across the man.

He lay tangled amid seaweed, his hair sand-grimed, his clothing drenched. For a moment she thought him drowned. Then his chest moved.

Shalindra stepped back a pace. Whence could he have come, if not from the sea? The fingers that dug into the wet sand were unwebbed, and the last merfolk had vanished years ago. No visitors came to Tyreen since the glacier had sealed Icehold Pass. This was no merman, but neither was he of her country. His rough dun tunic was of foreign cut, and he was stockier than folk from hereabouts.

He took another shallow breath. *Too slow.* Shalindra nerved herself to touch his hand. Icy, and his lips were blue. She shook his shoulder; his head lolled. After an eternity he breathed again.

She could see no hurt, yet he would not wake. In wintertime she'd seen folk stumbling with cold, wits

slowed enough that they eventually lay down to sleep forever. She shook him again. No response.

Panicked, she looked about. This was taking valuable time. In earlier days she could have warmed him with spells, wakened him, set his blood moving, but she no longer carried charms now that magic was fading. She could abandon him—*no*. Evil would spring from such a deed. She sighed.

She needed strong muscles. Not far off was Gilm's cottage. The carpenter and his grown son could help carry the stranger home. She ran and beat on the door.

Gilm swung it open. He grumbled about the stiffness in his back and hands, but he and his son came. They lifted the man as if he were a kitten.

Shalindra went ahead to make things ready. She must light a fire, gather blankets, brew tea, anything to restore warmth.

Up the ramp to the College, where merfolk formerly squelched from the water, bearing fish and sunken treasures; she spared scarcely a glance for the dragons that flanked the gate. Once they had gleamed with iridescent scales: now legs, tail, and trunk were dull gray. They had almost turned to stone. One bent its head as she passed.

The library was the only building that had not slumped to rubble. Here Shalindra and Llangru made their home, amid moldering books no one else could read.

She pushed open the door—its rusting hinges creaked—and stopped, surprised. Already fire blazed, a kettle steamed, and the long copper tub gleamed on the hearth. Llangru was holding blankets near the heat. He looked up when he saw her. His hands twitched, and the blankets tumbled.

His eyes sought the outlander. Strange eyes, they were, gray-blue bordered with paleness. They were often dreamy, but at this moment seemed intent. "I watched you find him, Mother," the boy said. "I knew you'd want warmth. Is he badly hurt?"

Shalindra frowned, puzzled, but voiced no question as Gilm and his son shuffled through the door. "Where you want him, lady?" Gilm growled.

"Over there, near the fire."

They set the man down and backed away, casting fearful glances at the shadows. "It's a cruel cold day for m' hands," Gilm hinted.

"Thank you for your help," said Shalindra. The two left as quickly as they could. She bent over the victim; he still breathed shallowly. "Help me strip him," she ordered Llangru, then bit her lip as the boy fumbled at fastenings. *Keep silence, it's not his fault he was born that way.* "Better yet, fetch more blankets."

It was difficult for a frail woman to remove his clothing—he lay a dead weight—but at last she heaped the sodden garments on the floor. Where sun had not seared him, his skin gleamed white. She had not seen an unclad man since Zaerrui died—and that was ten years gone, while she was pregnant with Llangru.

This man was of ordinary height, shorter by far than Zaerrui, but he would weigh as much or more: powerful muscles bulged arms, shoulders, and thighs. His chest was broad. He must be used to heavy work. Square-jawed and blunt-nosed, his features were somewhat rugged. In the manner of the Southerners, he wore his brown hair short, and was accustomed to shave his beard, though several days' worth of stubble showed.

"Help me lift him," Shalindra told Llangru. Mother and son strained, and finally eased the stranger into the steaming tub. "More hot water."

First came shivering, then awareness returned. The man opened gray eyes. She answered his unspoken question: "You are in the town of Tyreen, in the old College library where I make my home. I found you on the beach, half-dead. Who are you, and whence from?"

The cracked lips parted. She leaned forward to catch the words: "I am Brandek. I was on a ship, trying to—teach men—" He swallowed. Yes, his accent was Southern. In the years before the pass closed, folk from Aeth had often visited the College to confer with Zaerrui.

"Never mind talking," Shalindra said. She helped him from the tub, wrapped him in warm blankets, and fed him hot tea. "You can tell us all about it later."

He slipped into slumber. Shalindra thought she might leave Llangru on watch, and go back to the beach, but suddenly Gilm knocked on the door.

The old carpenter grinned, held out the sea-unicorn horn, and said, "See what I found on the strand, lady. It's yours in trade for a bit of magic."

"Thank you," Shalindra said. "What do you wish?"

He spread knotted fingers. "It's m' hands and back, they pain me sore. Make the hurt go away, an' I'll give ye this pretty thing."

Shalindra held the horn. White, slender, spiral, it was heavy with *mana.* Any fool could see that. "Very well," she said, "sit down."

The healing spell would not last, and Gilm would complain he had been cheated, if she did not add something special. For a few moments she admired the flawless beauty of the horn, before picking up a rasp. She felt almost physical anguish as she scraped. There, that much should suffice. She measured out the usual herbs and powdered pearl, and mixed the medicine with wine. Zaerrui's wine. She whispered the activating spell and handed Gilm the goblet. "Here, drink. This will help for a time." She watched him gulp; she'd brewed it bitter.

After the carpenter left she picked up what remained of the horn, a great length, but flawed, now. She set it in the corner, against a stack of musty books. It no longer held power to help Llangru. Perhaps nothing did.

She looked down at Brandek. *The fault, stranger, is yours. There you lie. Were you worth it?*

The moon had swung through two full cycles when Brandek returned to Shalindra's home. First, as propriety required, he had moved elsewhere after he could walk again. The household of Kiernon the blacksmith had been glad to take him in for the sake of hearing about the world beyond Tyreen and its hinterland; no outlander had crossed these ever-narrowing horizons for years. The place was soon beswarmed by people just as eager for news. His vigor regained, Brandek set about earning his keep. When he learned how lacking in huntsman's skills

they were hereabouts, though big game was fre-
quently seen, he offered to lead forth a party of young
men and teach them something. First, he discovered,
it was necessary to prepare weapons for the chase,
mainly spears, knives, and slings. With metal become scarce and precious, he chipped stone into
points and edges, an art he had seen practiced in
wild parts of the South but must largely re-invent
himself. Thereafter he must drill his would-be followers in the use of these things. At last they were
ready.

Their band was gone so long that kinfolk worried,
for it made countless mistakes—but it learned from
them, and came home triumphant.

Next day Brandek laid across his shoulder a
haunch of venison that he had smoked in the field.
Stepping out of Kiernon's door, he turned toward the
abandoned College of Wizards where Shalindra
dwelt alone with her son.

It was a bleakly bright summer morning. Wind
harried white clouds through the sky so that their
shadows and its whistling swept through grass-
grown, ruin-lined streets. Gray-green with glacial
flour, the Madwoman River poured noisily into a bay
where whitecaps danced on water the hue of steel.
On the southern bank, rubble heaps and snags of
towers marked the totally abandoned half of Tyreen.
There had been no sense in anyone living across the
stream after the bridge collapsed and only rafts were
available. Beyond lay the country where Brandek
had been hunting. Often he had spied fallen buildings in those reaches, for that had once been a land
of great plantations. Now it was tundra and taiga,

bearing naught but grass, moss, dwarf birch and willow, gnarled shrubs. They called it the Barren in Tyreen, and no one in living memory had gone far into it—for what could a man find there to keep himself alive?

Brandek struck out northerly through the town. The village, rather, he thought: just a few hundred souls remained. After weather spells failed and the glaciers marched south, while pests and murrains that were no longer checked by magic ravaged the farms, famine had taken off most of the population. Disease, cold, storm, fighting for scraps accounted for others. Eventually a certain balance had been struck, but everyone who could think knew how precarious it was.

Kiernon's house was better than most. Being clever with his hands, the smith had shored up a crumbling structure, even made an addition of timbers salvaged from tenantless places, roughly dovetailed together and chinked with mud. He had ample time for that, since no new iron ever came in and implements were wearing out, rusting away, or getting lost. (Still, the demand for repairs, paid for in kind, was sufficient to keep his family reasonably well off.) Striding along, Brandek passed dwellings that were little more than caves grubbed out of wreckage, or lean-tos against remnant walls. The bright colors of bricks, the occasional grace of a colonnade, the vividness of a phoenix in a mosaic of which half was gone, somehow made the scene doubly forlorn.

What people he met were less miserable than their surroundings . . . thus far. They were of his own race, though usually lighter-complexioned, sometimes blond, and might have been taller than him had not undernourishment stunted growth. However, they were wiry, and his young hunters had not lacked endurance. Their clothes, such as he necessarily wore, would have seemed archaic in Aeth—tunic and trousers for men, long gowns for women, hooded cloaks for both sexes—but were, after all, generally old, when wool and linen were in short supply; if dyes had faded, the patching and darning were carefully done.

Brandek did not encounter many persons. Most were out tending their meager fields and sparse flocks, gathering firewood, fishing along the river and bay shores. Those who stayed behind were children, housewives, the aged, the sick, the rare artisan like Kiernon. They hailed him in friendly wise. The meat he had gotten made him a hero.

"Hoy, my son told me how you tied a rack of antlers off a reindeer skull to your head, and threw a skin over your back, and went on all fours to within spearcast of the herd," said Hente the weaver. "And that hooked stick of yours for throwing the spear, he claims it doubles the range and force. Won't you show the rest of us?"

"Of course," Brandek replied, a bit curtly. He was impatient to be on his way. "You've a whale of a lot to learn here."

"A what? A whale of a lot? Hee, hee! That's a clever 'un. A Southern turn of speech, eh?" Hente cocked his head and regarded the burly man closely. "You're settling down for good, then, are you?"

Brandek shrugged. "I've no choice. Therefore I'd better do what I can to make this place fit to live in."

"Hoy, you're a gruff 'un, aren't you?" Hastily, Hente smiled. "Um, you'll be wanting a wife, and my daughter Risaya—well, I think you might like meeting her."

""No doubt. Later." Brandek nodded and went on. Hente stared after him. The weaver had little else to do, these days, and hunger was often a guest at his board.

Crossing Searoad, Brandek reached the College. Well-nigh all its proud buildings had fallen; he could look across weedy grounds and the ruins and hovels beyond, to city walls in nearly as bad repair. He cursed under his breath, not for the first time. Like any prosperous, populous community, Tyreen had made lavish use of magic. Indeed, because of this institution in its midst, it had been still more prodigal of *mana* than most were. When enchantments began to fail, so did the delicate, fantastic works, or the massive ones, which they had upheld against gravity and weather. Knowledge was lacking of how to rebuild in mundane fashion. The rot had gnawed less far inward in his homeland, but he had seen it there too—yes, in Aeth itself, which had been the capital of an empire that reckoned Tyreen a rich provincial town.

One hall of the College survived, in part. Ivy crawled over amber-hued masonry, would pry it asunder in due course, meanwhile hid friezes and inscriptions. Windows gaped glassless or were crudely boarded up. A fountain before the entrance held rainwater in its basin but did not spring any more, and its statue of a dancing maiden was lichenous and blurred. Nevertheless, here was shelter of a sort for many books, and for Shalindra and her boy.

Llangru sat on the stairs, rocking to and fro. His gaze was vacant and he did not seem to notice the newcomer. He was towheaded, handsome of face, but small and thin for his nine or ten years of age, unkempt despite everything his mother could do.

Brandek found her in the library, reading. A sunbeam like a flickery swordblade came in an ogive window and fell on time-browned pages; in that light, those shadows, the volumes shelved behind seemed to stir, and the sound of the wind was as if they sighed. Wrapped in a cloak against the chill, her slight form was hidden from him. He saw only a finely shaped face, large brown eyes, waist-length cataract of russet hair.

"Oh—" She peered nearsightedly before recognition came. Well, he thought, she'd scarcely seen him since he left her. "Brandek of Aeth! What do you wish?"

"To give you this," he said. The nearby table being piled high with tomes, he laid the meat down on the carpetless, stone-flagged floor. "I reckoned you could use it."

"Why—" She rose, stooped over and handled it, straightened and looked at him in wonder. "I know not how to thank you."

"No thanks needed, lady," he growled. "You saved my life, didn't you?" He paused, forcing himself, before he could add: "I hope I gave no offense. If I did, well, I was newly hauled from the sea and half out of my head from grief at lost shipmates and, and, everything."

"Oh, no, you never did," she murmured.

"Then why—I mean, everybody else wanted to hear what I could tell of the South. You never came to listen. Why not?"

She winced. Her gaze dropped. "I . . . don't like crowds." He could barely hear her. "Llangru would have wanted to come along, and . . . too many of them have been cruel to him . . . because he is different. . . . I kept hoping you would visit us."

"I should have, but it seemed I was always busy, finding my way around, getting things set up for that hunt, and then off on it—Shalindra, I came as soon as I could, honestly." Brandek smote fist into palm. The noise cracked loud through the dusty stillness. "But you—they—they're so *ignorant!* They don't see what's under their noses. And chaos take it, this is a survival matter. I'll have to live here too, you know. And I admit I'm not a very patient man."

She smiled and touched his arm. "Well, you came. Now I can hear your story at leisure, as I'd wanted to. Sit down." She pointed to an elaborately carved chair opposite hers. "I'll brew us a pot of tea—No." She laughed, and the clarity of that sound challenged the gloom around them. "I've some wine left that my husband made. Noble stuff; I swear that whatever magic he used has not gone out of *it*. A guest from Imperial Aeth, who's brought such a magnificent gift, yes, surely this is worth a small bottle."

In addition, she fetched bread and cheese—not much, for she had little—and she and Brandek settled down to a lively conversation. They had heard something about each other from third parties, but this was their first chance to become really acquainted.

Brandek was shorter-spoken. "I was a younger son

of a baron at home. It's barons and petty kings there; the Empire is just a memory. The climate is milder than here, but not notably, and worse every year. I saw things falling apart, the same as they've already done for you, and wondered what to do about it. Hunting—hunting was always a pleasure of mine, and I learned a lot from the wild tribes that've drifted into the Homptoleps Forest, these past hundred years. But I also thought we might try reviving coastwise shipping, get in contact with lost provinces, start trade again and—Well, I had a ship built and headed north, exploring. Without magic, she proved unseaworthy, for the wrights had small skill. She foundered in the storm, outside Tyreen Bay. I clung to a plank, and that's all I remember till I woke up in your care. Everybody else must have drowned." He grimaced. "No way for me to return, hey? North and east, the mountain passes are choked by the glaciers. South, the Barren is too wide; it's rich in wildlife close by, but I found that farther on it's still almost empty and a man would starve before he got across. So here I am."

Shalindra told her story at greater length, though there was actually less of it. Her husband, Zaerrui, had been the dean of the College, a wizard as learned and accomplished as the dwindling of *mana* in the world allowed. She was his tenth wife, for he was centuries old and had never been able, in this gaunt age, to cast a longevity spell on anyone else. Yet he and Shalindra were happy, and she was carrying their firstborn when suddenly the enchantment that kept him young guttered out and—She did not care to talk about that. Since, she had lived by the scant magic, ever less, that she commanded, and by trading off possessions for food, and by what work she could get as a scribe or clerk or the like; she was nearly the last literate person in Tyreen.

Mostly, talking with Brandek, she sounded him out about the South, as her fellow townsfolk had done. Did she press him too closely, or did he simply feel too deep a wound? He could not say. He only knew that at last he exclaimed: "The demons take that! Cities, books, riches, peace, leisure, yes, farms, metals—they're done! They're going the way the magic has gone, and you'll go too if you don't learn how to live in the world we've got."

She stiffened in her chair. "What do you mean?"

"You people! Fumbling around on your niggard acres, with your starveling livestock, when more and more big game is moving south ahead of the glaciers, elk, reindeer, boar, horse, aurochs, wisent, mammoth. . . . Your trying to patch up junkheaps like, like this building, when you could find out how to make shelters that're warm and weather-tight." His fist struck his knee. "I tried to give the old world new life, by my ship. The sea taught me better. Now I've got to teach all of you!"

Shocked, she whispered, "Do you mean we should give up our whole civilization—all the old ways—and become savages? No!" Pride straightened her back and squared her shoulders. "Quit if you wish, Brandek. I had expected more from a man of Aeth, but do as you will. I, though, I am a sorceress in my own right, the wife of the dean of the College—yes, *still* his wife—and mother of his son. No, I'll not betray that heritage. Nor will Llangru after me."

They glared at each other before changing the subject. He left as soon as decently possible, and their parting was cool.

Autumn was drawing to a close, and Shalindra dreaded the coming season. Rain-raw wind whined through the windows, and the College fountain brimmed with sodden leaves. Snowdrifts soon would smother Tyreen. Each year the frost fell earlier.

As always, when cold crept down the stone halls, Llangru sickened. Formerly Shalindra's medicines could soothe the rattle in his chest and cool his fever, but of late they availed little. Each winter's illness left him more weakened. Even in summer he coughed. If only, Shalindra thought, they could stay warm and dry . . .

Today he lay flushed, eyes bright, staring at something his mother could not see. He held out his arms, spread his fingers, and chanted, "Soaring, over glittery waves, fish like silver needles. Winds cradle me. Tyreen lies tiny, far down. The boys romp in the street. I could stoop on them, but why bother? It's cool and blue here, the sun warms my wings, the fish below me dance for joy—"

Shalindra sponged his forehead. He often babbled thus, claiming to be a hawk, a fox, once a great shambling bear—Llangru, who had never walked the Barren or the forest. He had merely seen wild animals in books. Llangru spent his life cowering in the library, hidden from the jeers and taunts of normal children. The townsfolk knew him to be sincere in his claims, so they thought him mad. *Had Zaerrui lived, could he have helped his son?*

The boy needed fruit, fresh vegetables, milk—for perhaps the twentieth time that day, Shalindra opened her larder. The shelves gleamed bare. One hook, amid an empty dozen, held a shoulder of smoked elk: a gift from Brandek. Its gamy taste was strange to one used to fat beef cattle. Yet it was the sole meat Shalindra had, and she was grateful for whatever Brandek did to preserve it. Long ago, spoilage was no problem; a simple spell kept meat and produce fresh. But over time, magic had faded. She remembered going to her larder one morning to fix Zaerrui a festive breakfast; she had opened the door and gagged at corruption.

Now her problem was finding anything to eat. Brandek brought food, sometimes a silent leaving on the doorstep, but charity made a bitter meal.

Tyreen ate better, though; Brandek was teaching his hunting band new ways. Kiernon's son Destog, for instance, scorned to work in metal. He'd fashioned a spear and hunted for a living. The spearpoint was flint. Brandek's work, likewise. Knives made by Destog's father lay broken and rusted.

Again Shalindra examined the shelves. She might have overlooked something. The smoked meat, part of a cheese, a crust of bread—that was all. Most of her possessions she had bartered away. Last to go were the carved chair, her ivory boxes, the circlet that once bound her hair. Naught remained but the books. She would not part with those. Had she wished to, they were valueless. Tyreen no longer wanted even a writing of births, deaths, and marriages.

Shalindra raised her hands to her face. Her last gold bracelet slid down a thin arm. *No, I'll not trade that. Not Zaerrui's wedding gift.* It would buy food for a short time, but soon that, too, would be eaten. *So what's to do? I'm scarcely a sorceress any longer.*

Old Abba, for instance, was among her failures: Shalindra had helped her for years, until abruptly the potions no longer worked. The laundress had sickened and died in weeks. Her family thought Shalindra had willfully held back magic. *But there is no magic left. At least not in me.*

An idea struck her. She laughed, a choking sound, quickly stifled. She did not wish to rouse Llangru. Since Abba's death, Tyreen lacked a laundress. Well, Shalindra did know how to make soap, and washing was an honorable task, not like being someone's kept woman, or worse. The townsfolk might not need a scribe, but they did need clean clothes.

She dragged out the big copper tub and inspected it. Dents and spots worn thin were plentiful, but it should hold together for a while. She checked on Llangru a final time and set forth seeking work.

Shalindra knelt by the tub, scrubbing. Llangru, a book propped on his lap, read aloud. On demand he could fetch more hot water, but he was too clumsy for any real labor.

The shirt she washed was patched. How long since anyone had had strong new linen, cotton, wool? Hente the weaver sat idle. His sons had joined Brandek's band, and fed their parents.

Llangru read on: "To ensure fair weather for a festival, take clippings from the mane of a white unicorn, the oily tears of a merchild, and, in an amethyst flask, gather dragon's breath. On the night of the dark moon mix these together—"

Shalindra lifted the shirt. How long since unicorns pranced or merfolk swam, how long since the College's guardian dragons had last moved?

Gently, she wrung out soapy water. The shirt came apart in her hands. Rough hands, work-reddened; no longer the fingers Zaeurri had kissed.

Cloth garments were vanishing. Brandek and his hunters wore animal hides, harsh on the skin and clumsily-sewn. She looked at the blue fabric of her gown. It hung soft against her body, draped in pleasing folds, but the hem was threadbare and the sleeves were patched.

She wiped a soapy arm across her eyes, lest Llangru see her tears.

Day at midwinter was brief and pale in this land, when clouds did not make twilight of it or snowstorms strike men with white blindness. Brandek could seldom go to sleep at nightfall or sit quietly in the house he had occupied. It was too cold and dark. He had been using odd moments to carve fat-burning lamps out of soapstone, but as yet he had only three. Hence he became a frequenter of the last tavern in Tyreen. The magical light-globes there were extinct too, but you needed no more than hearth-glow to drink by. Besides, he usually enjoyed the company; and if nothing else, it was well to be friendly, for some people resented his rapid rise to dominance.

One night was frozenly clear. A full moon cast long shadows from the east and made the snow sheen and glisten. Beneath it he saw the peaks of the Heewhirlas thrust whiter still above the horizon.

Elsewhere, stars thronged heaven and the Silver Torrent cataracted in the same silence that made the scrunch of his boots on the snow seem loud. His breath went ghostly before him.

The cold slid fingers past his garments. Fur and leather were better than cloth, but none of the men who tried had yet perfected the art of preparing these materials, nor had any woman—in this case, Hente's daughter Risaya, anxious to impress the great hunter —grown skillful at making clothes from them. Well, that would come with experience, Brandek knew. He hefted the flint-headed spear he carried, and his free hand dropped to the obsidian knife at his hip. Several men, himself included, were already good at shaping stone.

So much to learn, discover, master—A sigh sent Brandek's breath flying. He often thought that the existence of *mana* had finally proven more a curse than a blessing. When it was exhausted through use, mankind knew very little else. Without it, the race would have developed techniques which depended only on the enduring aspects of the world. For instance, there must be a better way to light a dwelling than by a wick afloat in a bowl of grease; but no one was likely to hit upon any when countless different inventions were more urgently needed.

He saw the Green Merman ahead and lengthened his stride. The tavern was formerly the house of someone who could not pay magicians to help in the construction. Hence it abided, though much decayed in the timbers, amidst hillocks which had been more pretentious neighbors. Light seeped dim around the edges of warped door and shutters. Smoke billowed from a hole in the roof, where tiles had been removed when spells no longer kept weather balmy.

Wolves began to howl. They sounded like a large pack, and right outside the North Gate. Belike they were in quest of livestock; it was becoming impossible to keep herds or flocks safe from predators. More than once Brandek had raged at the owners, that they wasted time trying when the coastal plain and the mountains held abundant wild game.

Their sons usually agreed with him, and that had broken several families, and that had earned him added reproaches by Shalindra. Brandek flung the tavern door wide and stamped in. "Red wine, a mug of it!" he roared.

The air made his eyes and lungs sting. Just four men clustered at the single table, amidst unrestful thick shadows. Money was meaningless, and few could spare goods to swap for the diminishing store of drink. Brandek had ample credit from the pelts he brought out of the wilderness, and endeared himself to chosen fellow patrons by treating them.

Tonight they spoke no welcome but sat tense. Even muffled by walls, it was as if the sudden wolf-howls had pierced them. Terbritt the landlord must swallow before he could say, huskily, "I'm sorry. No more wine."

"What?" Brandek was astounded. "I've seen—"

"Yes, sir, two barrels were left. After that, no more wine, ever. And Jayath, the chirurgeon, you know, he and a lot of others came to tell me it should be kept for those who're in pain or need his knife. The Lord Mayor's taken charge of it."

Brandek uttered an oath, then curbed his temper.

For the most part, city government had become a solemn farce. He, the outlander, had already gained more real power, merely by showing people how to survive and browbeating them into doing so. He had still less faith in the chirurgeon; fate deliver him from ever falling into those untrained hands!

However, many did trust Jayath, and the belief doubtless strengthened them. Therefore turning the wine over to him was a move toward solidarity, in this divided and demoralized community.

"All right," Brandek said. "Beer will do. It'd better."

Nobody chuckled. He settled down on a bench next to Gilm the carpenter, who mumbled, "Soon no more beer, either. Drink it while it's there." He had obviously been setting an example. With abrupt violence, he banged his goblet on the table. "I got credit. Gave Terbritt the two halves of a saw after it broke today. Next to last saw in my kit. Terbritt says he'll have Kiernon turn it into knives. No way to make a new saw, o' course. Who needs cabinets or cedar chests any longer, anyway? Houses? Why, the wood we can pull out o' the ruins is generally rotten, and the Northern forests are under the glacier, and no ships bring timber from the South." He hiccoughed. "My son began in my trade too, you remember. He'll not end in it. No call for carpenters. What'll he *do?*"

Brandek clapped the man's shoulder. "Let him learn hunting, or stone-chipping, or any of a host of crafts that really are needed. I'll be glad to teach him what I can."

"Teach him to be a . . . a savage!"

The wolf chorus, which had quieted, broke forth

again. Wisnar, who farmed, traced a sign across his broad breast. His beard fell that far down; not many razors remained. (Brandek had acquired one and used it regularly, as a way of maintaining he was no enemy of civilization.) "What's that you do?" asked Lari, who had been a merchant and now lived by trading away what remained in his warehouses. Fear shrilled through his voice.

"I make the mark of my family," Wisnar told them, "hoping my forebears will guard me against yonder demons; for the gods died long ago."

The landlord stiffened where he stood tapping the beer. "Hold on," he exclaimed. "I'll not have another Alsken in this house."

Wisnar bridled, dread half lost in indignation. "I'm no such thing. You ought to know me better than that, all of you."

"An Alsken?" asked Brandek. "What do you mean?"

Anxious to smooth matters over, Terbritt said fast: "Alsken was a man of this town, a few years ago, who claimed he had found a stone so full of *mana* that he was now as mighty a sorcerer as . . . as Zaer-rui was of old. Many believed him, and in their need showered him with gifts and did his every bidding. But then it was found he had nothing more, really, than sleight of hand and other such tricks. A mob tore him apart, and the building he was in as well. I'm sorry, Wisnar. I spoke too fast. You're no charlatan like that, I'm sure. I was only anxious lest the Green Merman suffer."

The farmer shook his head. "No, I'm no fraud, I make no claims for myself. I told you what I did—

beseech, just beseech my forefathers to help me. It may well be that they're bones in their graves, as dead as magic itself. But—" He grimaced as if in pain. "But what harm in calling on them, when we who live are helpless against those demons out there?"

"Those?" Brandek protested. "They're only wolves."

"Only!" Wisnar yelled. "If you knew their cunning, if you knew the harm they've wrought me—If they aren't demons themselves, then they're possessed. And what shall stand between us and them?"

"But I'd not call on ghosts for help," Lari quavered. "Who knows what ghosts might want?"

A shudder ran around the table. Terbritt's hand slopped the beer he set down before Brandek. The wolves howled louder. From afar, a mammoth trumpeted. A groan arose, and two men covered their eyes.

Aged Fyrlei alone sat as still as the Southerner. Once he had been the town's interpreter for the last of the merfolk who came trading; he had been accustomed to the unhuman. Yet it could be seen that he thrust his quietness upon himself, and what he said was: "The magic is gone. But muster your courage, lads, the courage to hope that Our Father of the Tusks will be merciful to us."

"Would he take an offering, do you think?" Lari asked.

Brandek's fist crashed on the board. "Let him offer to us!" he answered, deep in his throat. "A walking hoard of meat, bone, hide, ivory—You dread him simply because his kind has very lately come down from the North. What other cause is there? Stop quaking at every change that happens along, and use your common sense." He made a spitting noise. "If you have any."

"Too much has changed, too soon," Terbritt said, and slumped down onto the bench.

"Aye," Fyrlei murmured, "everything now is unknown. We're like sailors on a rudderless boat adrift in a fog. Nothing is left us but courage, and it must stand naked."

"Then don't weaken it by whimpering," Brandek snapped at them all.

His words did not lash them into a healthy anger as he wished. They sat huddled in their terror. Wisnar did retort, with dull resentment, "You're no help yourself, fellow. You throw your weight around like a legate of the Empire. But the Empire's dust on the wind, and what you really do is turn our children against us."

"I try to show them how Tyreen can best survive," Brandek said in a milder tone. He would not openly admit what he realized, that he was often too overbearing. Such was his nature, and the terrible plight of these people did not make him patient with fecklessness.

"Yes, like that boy in your hunting party who met his death last month," Wisnar answered.

"He saw something strange at the riverside, where we were," Brandek explained for the dozenth time. "He panicked, bolted off, went through thin ice, and drowned before we could reach him. The strange thing turned out to be no more than another beast new to these parts—a rhinoceros, we'd call it in Aeth,

213

though this was woolly—a calf, at that, surely strayed from its mother." He did not remind them that a third of his band had refused to help kill the animal, and later nobody at home would touch the valuable carcass. They supposed a nameless evil force must be in it, and knew not how to cope.

He had requested aid of Shalindra. She could pretend to cast a spell and annul the curse. Appalled, she refused to debase the art which had been her husband's and her own. Let it lie honorably in its grave. Besides, who could tell what misfortune might indeed come of a thing which had already claimed one life? He had snarled and stamped off. Inwardly, almost reluctantly, he mourned that this had further widened the rift between them.

Fyrlei nodded his white head. "Aye, Brandek, you mean well and you do well," he said. "You show us ways of coping with the material world, ways we'd never have thought of by ourselves. However, you are no visionary. You spoke of common sense. How can that exist when *nothing* makes sense any more?"

The question pierced. The old man had wisdom of a sort. If the heart went altogether out of them, whatever skills they gained, the folk of Tyreen would not have long to live.

Brandek's hand closed on his crude wooden goblet, as though to splinter it. The wolves and the mammoth chanted through the night around him.

A warm spring breeze scurried into the courtyard, bearing a whiff of Brandek's latest project. He had discovered some new way to cure hides. In Shalindra's opinion, the stench was even more offensive than in the old method of scraping and drying.

Hente, the weaver, grieved at the advent of leather garments, but since weather-spells had failed, the flax crops were blighted. Wolves, driven south before the ice, harried the sheep and made wool unobtainable. Folk simply had no way to produce cloth. Hente's youngest son tanned skins for a living.

Shalindra poured hot water into the fountain and started a wash. Little enough work was left for her; each week more clothes fell to tatters.

The pleasant morning had tempted Llangru out of the compound. She let him go; she could not shelter him forever. Already he stood nearly as tall as his mother. In a few years he would shoot up into manhood.

What life will there be for him, then? Her son lacked the brute strength to face this world.

Soft-shod feet shuffled across cobbles. She turned and gasped. Llangru's face was a sheet of gore. His tunic flapped over skinned knees, and his knuckles were raw. Tears had traced dirty paths down his cheeks. Behind him loomed Brandek, dressed for the hunt.

Shalindra sprang forward. "What have you done to him?" she shrilled, though she knew the question was stupid. Brandek did not harm children.

"It's only a bloody nose," the Southerner said. "They always look dramatic. It's mostly stopped running. Wash your face, young man. You've scared your mother."

Llangru nodded gravely and stepped over to the fountain. It was full of laundry, so he cupped water

215

in his palms. Last winter Shalindra's copper tub had holed through. No one knew how to patch it. The fountain, which was granite, endured. The dancing maiden's outstretched hand held a bowl of fat-and-ash soap.

Shalindra watched the worst of the blood rinse away. Brandek was right, the injuries were minor. She was ashamed of her outburst. "Come inside," she said, "and you both can tell me what happened."

Brandek sat on the floor, his back against a pile of books. Most of Shalindra's furniture was gone, broken or traded. He gulped herb tea from a fragile ceramic cup. Around its rim writhed red-and-golden dragons. Llangru and Shalindra drank from wooden mugs.

"I was walking out Searoad, by the market, when I heard shouting. There was Llangru in a knot of older boys—six of them, but he was putting up a good fight. I think Mintu led them, as usual. He's the one with the loud mouth. I should take that bully out hunting aurochs—if he brings a good supply of dry breeks!"

Llangru, who sat between his mother and Brandek, nodded. "It was Mintu. He didn't like what I said."

"I've told you not to get into arguments with those boys," Shalindra began, but Llangru cut her off.

"Mintu was telling lies. He said he'd gone hunting alone and killed an elk. It was too big to drag home, and a pack of wolves ate it. He killed most of them, too. He said he was every bit as good a hunter as Brandek, and knew how to chip sharper spearpoints.

I couldn't let him go on bragging like that, so I told them I'd seen what really happened."

Shalindra frowned. Her son often had wild fancies.

He continued: "Mintu never killed any elk. He's scared to be out alone, and he made so much noise in the woods that even the weasels were laughing. He found an elk that had been dead since last fall. They don't even *have* antlers in the spring." He looked up at Brandek. "You know that; you told me."

The man nodded.

"It was by the river, upstream, mostly just bones. He'd borrowed his father's saw. He finally cut one antler loose, but he was too lazy to take the other, so he left it and came back with a made-up story. I saw it all."

"Llangru," Shalindra said, "how far upstream was this, did you say?"

"Most of a morning's walk, for Mintu. I flew."

"You flew." Shalindra's tone was flat.

"Of course. I was an eagle. I like that. You can see everything, and swoop down on rabbits, but I feel sorry for them, they squeal so. You can soar with the sun warm on your wings and the world tiny down below. The roof on the library is gray-green, and tiles are missing on the west wing, where the ceiling leaks. You can hardly *see* the dragon statues—" His eyes were brilliant.

Shalindra slapped him. Llangru's head rocked back; his nose dripped fresh crimson. Aghast, Shalindra looked at her blood-smeared palm. "I, I shouldn't have struck you, dear," she stammered. "But you shouldn't tell stories."

"That's what Mintu said, before they beat me."

Llangru set down his mug and shuffled from the room.

Silence settled, broken only by fire-hiss and the boom of a wind turning raw. Brandek frowned but held his peace, while Shalindra stared into the depths of her mug. The wood was warped and cracking. He had told her hot liquids caused that, and added with a laugh that the tavern had no such problem. Well, he swilled enough of its beer—

Finally Brandek spoke. "The business was more serious than Llangru told you. Those boys were afraid. They were ready to tear him apart for being different. If I hadn't come along they might have killed him. I don't know what I think of his story, but they half believed it, Mintu most of all."

"Llangru has always been a strange one," Shalindra admitted. If she gazed straight ahead, into the fire, she could almost imagine that Zaerrui sat in his accustomed chair. But if she looked he would not be. And the chair was gone too, traded off last autumn. She gulped. "Maybe it's my fault. Llangru's father died before he was born." She bit her lip.

"Tell me," Brandek urged.

Shalindra was about to refuse, but words spilled forth: "It was a fine fall day eleven years ago. We were expecting a guest from Olanna, beyond the mountains. Zaerrui and the scholar wished to confer on why magic was fading, and whether anything might bring it back.

"We flew to meet the party at Icehold Pass. It was an easy journey, Zaerrui on his great black griffin, I on my winged unicorn.

"The air was crisp as apples. We raced, and arrived before our guests. As we landed, we could see them far off down the road. The scholar did not care to fly, so his group moved more slowly. While we waited, I told Zaerrui what I'd learned by divination that morning: I was carrying his son.

"He whooped for joy: *We'll name him Llangru!* He spun me a veil of sunbeams, and wove a crown of golden leaves. A simple magic, that. Only a small, simple magic." She swallowed. She dared not weep.

"Then it happened. Zaerrui clutched his chest. His hair bleached white, and his face wrinkled. He gasped one word: *Run.* I did not want to leave him; he hurled a lightning bolt, and my mount screamed and took flight. His own griffin stood like black stone. I looked back once to see the mountains slump and the glacier grind green ice across the pass; then my unicorn fluttered earthward like an autumn leaf, and died.

"When I reached Tyreen, my feet were bleeding, and I was half-starved. The town had fallen to rubble. Folk crouched amid wreckage. Snow howled early that year. When spring came, the pass did not open.

"I took shelter in the College library, and here I bore Llangru, Zaerrui's last son."

Silence, again. A gust through an empty window fluttered some sheets of paper that lay on the table, weighted down by a useless scrying stone. Shalindra had been practicing calligraphy, lest her work stiffen her fingers till she also lost that equally useless art.

"And was Llangru always—the way he is?" Brandek's question was soft.

"Yes," she said. "He talked at the normal age—

nothing wrong with his mind—but he had trouble learning to feed himself and walk. I don't know the reason, or what went awry. It may be that the magic that wards babes has faded too."

"All magic is going, Shalindra, you know that. There was just so much in the world, and men used it up. We can only keep on, and in different ways. It won't be easy." Brandek leaned forward, almost touching her. "I have an idea I want to try this summer. Boats."

"You nearly died when your ship sank," the woman said, a trifle shocked. "Haven't you seen enough of the sea?"

"I dared too much. This time I'm minded to build small craft, not sailed but paddled, to venture no farther than the mouth of Tyreen Bay. We could do offshore fishing, and gather eggs on Geirfowl Island. Maybe, as our skill grows, we can advance to larger vessels and longer trips, begin re-opening coastwise trade routes—" He went on.

Shalindra merely half-listened, until he mentioned hides. She remembered the stench.

"I'm finding new ways of treating leather. We can already make it supple, for clothing, but now we can make it strong and waterproof as well. I can cover a wooden frame, lashed together, with skins smeared in grease. Given careful stitching, that should produce a reliable hull."

It was if Shalindra heard the drip, drip, drip from the west wing in every downpour. "Hides can keep water out?"

"Yes," said Brandek, "if first you cure them in—"

Excitement flared through her. "But that means I

can save the books! The damp is killing them! Look at that stack, I've been trying to dry them by the fire. The rain comes in through holes in the roof that nobody can repair. A watertight shelter—"

Brandek reached back and took a volume. The cover was black with mildew. He opened it; moisture had freckled the pages. "Longevity spells," he grunted, and shook his head. "Those haven't worked for years—generations, most places. What's the use?" He set the book on the floor.

Shalindra rose. Staggering under the weight, she returned it to the stack. "If you misfile an item in a library this size—" she gestured at shelves stretching endless down the gloom of halls beyond this chamber—"you have lost it."

Brandek shrugged. "And what if you have? I'm educated, like you, and you've taught your boy, but how many others in Tyreen care a belch about writing? You've told me how you couldn't find recent employment as a scribe. People are cold, hungry, and afraid. Better they learn to hunt, make tools, build shelters, not read crumbling books of worthless wizard-lore."

"Worthless wizard-lore!" The words stung Shalindra like a slap. "Barbarian! Would you make all men illiterate? Have them trust naught but half-remembered tales?"

Brandek flushed, gnawed his lip, and finally replied: "Haven't we squabbled about this often enough? Books were good to have once. Today . . . they might serve to start fires." He shook his head. "No, I can't spare you any hides for their shelter. We'll need all we can get, and then some, to make those coracles." His curbed anger broke loose and he almost shouted, "Or would you rather keep reading until everybody starves to death in this ice-trap that's got us?"

"Well I know," Shalindra said, word by word, "that the ice has us trapped. My Zaerrui's bones lie beneath it. Would that they were yours instead."

She turned her back. Brandek sprang up. She heard something crunch, and turned again. In his haste he had kicked his cup across the floor and it shattered, the fragile ancient cup for guests. She saw a dragon's eye gleam gold on one fragment, as if to cast a look of despair upon the world.

She held her tone steady. "So you've smashed that too, as you'd smash everything else that was ours. You'll never rest, will you, till you've ground the last spark of civilization under your heel and we're all filthy, stinking savages, hunkered in caves with blood on our hands. Tell me, Brandek, shall we still cook our meat then, or do you want us to forget about fire also?"

"You seemed well pleased to eat the meat I left here, while you huddled among your precious books," he growled, and snatched a volume from the nearest shelf. *A Dictionary of the Mer-Tongue.* How fine! What a shame the merfolk are gone!" He chose another at random. *Raising the Dead.* Yes, I can see how you'd like that, Shalindra. You're more at home with the dead than the living, no?" He dropped both tomes. The spines broke. Loose pages swirled across the room. "Meanwhile you take in laundry from the village. That's the best your sorcery can do for you, and you refuse to learn anything new." He drew an uneven breath. "Teeth of doom, woman, it's magic that is dead. Give it a decent burial and come alive again yourself!"

Shalindra knelt, gathering scattered paper. Her hands shook. Brandek was right, in his way: her powers were gone. How many more years could she do heavy labor? Tears blurred her vision, and she turned away.

There, in the corner, gleamed something white and slender. She remembered, suddenly, what it was. She surged to her feet and strode across the room.

The sea-unicorn's horn was long, heavier than it looked. She laid hold of the spiral-curved lance. "Get out," she said. "Get out. Take this with you. It was the price of your life. I made a poor bargain. This, at least, once held *mana*." She proffered it, point first. *He thinks I'll stab him.* She stifled a laugh.

His eyes narrowed; he touched the hilt of his knife, then let his hands fall, and backed away. He fumbled at the latch; the door creaked open. He gathered his spear, throwing-stick, and ax. In his furs, he looked like a savage. He began to say something. Shalindra threw the horn after him. It shattered on the cobbles beyond. "Take it, you barbarian," she screamed, "and begone!"

Llangru pushed past her. "Brandek, don't leave," the boy pleaded. Shalindra leaned against the wall, put an arm across her eyes, and wept.

She heard Llangru stumble after Brandek, calling. The man soon outdistanced him. Llangru called once more, gave up, and started back. Afar, a mammoth trumpeted, harbinger of the oncoming ice.

Cren, son of Wisnar, and Destog, son of Kiernon, waited as agreed outside the Great Gate. It was no longer much more than a hill of tumbled blocks, from which a sculptured head, noseless, stared blindly eastward. The youths were about the same age, probably twenty winters. Though Cren was blond and Destog dark, somehow they looked alike as they stood there. Perhaps it was their outfits, garb of fur-trimmed leather, spear in hand, throwing stick and knife tucked into belt, two extra spears and a sleeping bag and packet of dried meat secured by thongs across the back. Or perhaps it was their build. Undernourished in childhood, they shared a leanness which long tours on the hunt, after Brandek came, were turning rangy. In their eyes, too, was a feral quality Tyreen had never known before.

"What kept you, sir?" Cren asked.

"A spot of trouble. Never mind about that," Brandek snapped. Inwardly he recognized that it had been well to rescue Llangru, but wrong to dawdle with Shalindra when his followers expected him. Why had he done it? Did some remnant of witchcraft still cling to her? "Let's be off. The morning's already old."

"Where are we bound this time?" Destog inquired eagerly.

Brandek's plan had been to go after horse. A herd had been spied yesterday, north of here. A large party would alarm the beasts too early, but a few men, sound of wind and limb, could get sufficiently close that, when the creatures did bolt, they could run one down, driving it between them as wolves do. Lately he had been experimenting with a noose on a long cord, to cast around the neck of an animal, but this was a skill which would take a while to develop.

Now he looked east, away from the town, across miles whose emptiness was scarcely broken by a few tumbledown, abandoned farm buildings, until the snowpeaks of the Heewhirlas caught his glance. "Yonder," he said, with a gesture. Bear had become plentiful in the uplands. Newly roused from winter sleep, such a brute would be gaunt and savage, but nonetheless a prize. And he *needed* a fight.

The others were astonished. "Spring is a dangerous season in the mountains," Cren blurted. "Avalanches—"

Brandek fashioned a sneer. "Stay behind if you're afraid."

"I'm not!" Yet Cren added hesitantly, "It's just that you're always telling us yourself, sir, the chase is risky enough without taking chances we don't have to."

"But you mean we've got to discover how to get along in any kind of conditions, don't you, sir?" Destog's earnest question sealed the matter. Brandek felt he could hardly change his mind after it, though beneath the seething, a part of him regretted his impulse. Leading people starved for certitudes, he must always pretend to a kind of *mana* of his own.

He nodded and set forth at a steady lope. His disciples came behind. They could maintain the pace, with brief pauses, till evening, when it would have brought them well into the chaotic lands below the heights.

They could not spare breath for talk, however, and

Brandek found himself locked up with his thoughts.

All his spears were tied to his shoulders. He gripped the ax he bore until knuckles stood white. It was another experiment of his, a flint blade set through a haft. After numerous failures, he dared hope that the lashings of shrunken rawhide would keep stone wedded to wood; but only heavy use would show if he had really found his way to making a trustworthy tool.

Wedded—He might as well go ahead and marry Hente's daughter Risaya. She wasn't bad-looking, and she had acquired the necessary new skills faster than most. Of course, Kiernon's youngest had a fullness about her suggesting she'd be a lively bed-mate, as well as bearing him strong children . . . . They were chaste and monogamous in Tyreen, but he was the most desirable husband material they knew; and he must have offspring—daughters to bind him in family alliances, sons to aid him and in the end, if he lived to be old, care for him; and his loins often burned.

Curse Shalindra, anyhow! Too long had he buzzed about that slim body, that deep mind—no, that skinny, nearsighted, daydreaming jackdaw. Most of her childbearing years were behind her, too; she was doubtless good for three or four yet, but could expect to lose at least one in infancy . . . . Why should he care? She and her books and her useless brat—He was being unfair. Llangru couldn't help his own helplessness and bore it with a certain gallantry. But why had she and Brandek gone on, month after month, when nearly every meeting ended in a fight?

Well, whatever he owed her, he had paid back a

hundredfold; and today she herself had screamed that there never was any debt, and had flung the token of it at his feet.

Must she take so hard the breaking of a cup? How like her. Oh, yes, Brandek thought, it had been a pretty object and he was sorry. He even wished he could offer her a replacement, however crude; but his attempts to make vessels of fired clay, during the winter, had come to naught. That was evidently an art whose development would take more time than anyone could spare, these days, from creating the means of stark survival.

His bootsoles whispered on stone. At the Great Gate, Searoad became Aiphive Way and ran across the coastal plain, over Icehold Pass, to the rich province beyond . . . formerly. Without magical maintenance, rains washed out the shallow bed, thin paving blocks slid apart and roots of grass cracked them to bits, the thoroughfare was already a mere trace and in a century or two would be erased. For that matter, the pass had been choked on the day when Shalindra was widowed.

Brandek glanced about him. To right and left he glimpsed stumps. Orchards had been cut down for firewood after frost killed them. Everywhere else, the grass of springtime billowed, pale green, beneath a wind that came sliding chill off the ocean. The air was full of water and earthy odors. Clouds scudded white; their shadows scythed across the land. Birds clamored aloft in huge flocks. Brandek wondered if he could find a means to cast a dart that high. Ahead, the range shouldered above the horizon, blue-gray where it was not whitened. He made out that tower-like peak men called the Bridegroom. A scowl seized his brow. He turned off the dying road, toward a different height, around which ice crystals flurried and glittered, the one they called Ripsnarl.

At eventide, the party made camp below that mountain. Although they were well into the chaotic land by then, they heard wolves howl after sunset, and later a deep-throated roar.

Once the Heewhirlas had lifted sheer from the coastal plain. Legend said that a god had fashioned them thus, to create a dramatic pattern. But gods died and magic faded, and at last no force remained to uphold those forms. When they slumped, great chunks of them came crashing down to make a jumble below the remaining steeps. This wreckage provided some grazing for chamois, and ample dens for bear and cave lion. These sought most of their food in the outer parts, strewn across miles. There boulders the size of houses, or whole walls of them, gave weather-shelter to plant life that in turn nourished animals.

A night in such a coppice had not calmed Brandek. He had slept ill in his bag, quarreling with Shalindra in his very dreams. At dawn, he was brusque with his companions.

"We'll spend the day separately, in search of spoor," he told them. "We'll meet here before dark, exchange information, and lay our plans. Don't forget for a moment how easy it is to lose your way hereabouts. Keep taking bearings on peaks and sun, but don't trust them much; rain or fog or whatever can blot them out of your sight. So memorize landmarks as you go, and make marks where you can. If you do get lost, don't panic. Settle down, wait till you see the sky again, and work your way toward the west. You'll come out in the open eventually, and be able to locate this camp." He paused. "If not, we're better off without you."

They reddened at his unwonted condescension. Usually he had been genial and sympathetic, in his bluff fashion. "Yes, sir," Cren said, while Destog's features showed hurt. The young men took up their loose spears and went in different directions.

Brandek lingered for a bit. Oaths muttered from him. Half were aimed at himself. He was being a fool, he knew. What sense in taking out on those lads his fury at Shalindra? And what did it matter in the first place what she said or did? She and her weird boy—yes, that was why the children persecuted Llangru. A strangeness possessed him, and in a world from which the comforting, controlling, explaining *mana* had departed, strangeness was a terror, therefore an object of hatred. Those two were ghosts and did not know it. Then let her stop haunting him!

He spat and struck off on his own.

Scrub birch, nestled on the side of a granite windrow, fell behind. He wound and climbed among masses between whose somberness the shadows and the cold lay heavy. Mists drifted in streamers under a sky that was wan and splashed with cirrus clouds. The colors of lichen, clumps of grass, patches of moss fairly shouted, so rare were they. Now and then, somewhere, a raven croaked. Mechanically, Brandek recorded his location in his mind; but otherwise he wandered almost at random, scamping his search for signs of big game.

If only Shalindra—he thought. If only Shalindra—She was no weakling. He had to concede her that much. Look how she struggled to maintain herself. And she was bright, she could learn what she needed to learn. Doubtless she would never be the best cook or denkeeper that a huntsman might have; but she could, for instance, turn her gift for things like calligraphy toward the making of decorated garments for which neighbors would trade what they themselves brought forth, including help with everyday tasks .... Brandek's ax clove air. Forget her!

Seeking to do that, he harked back to Aeth, his city that he would never see again. He called forth palaces, parks, porticos, kinfolk, friends, populace—and found surprisingly little homesickness in his heart. The city was a crumbling shell; most of what few people remained grubbed the earth beyond its walls and had no hope; the few who kept a little wealth were as obsessed with the past as *she* was, if not more. It was his impatience with their sort, as much as anything else, which had driven him to make his expedition and thus at last to Tyreen. Here the future lay, here most were winning to a readiness to grapple with the world as it was, and he liked them for that. Why must she hold out, and why must he care?

A sunbeam struck between clouds to dazzle him. Suddenly he noticed that he had been scrambling for hours and was hungry. Yet that was not what halted him. It was something that, in the brightness, leaped forth at his attention.

Huntsman's habit made him look around before he examined the sight more closely. He was halfway

up a long slope on the lower flank of Ripsnarl. Grass and wildflowers grew in patches between scattered boulders. Well below him was a mossy hollow in among such rocks, intensely green against their gray. Ahead, the stone wilderness reared sharply toward a bank of talus beneath darkling palisades; above those, wind-whirled crystals of dry snow, wherein rainbow fragments danced, hid the spike of the mountain. He heard the air yowling up there.

What stood immediately before him was a mass twice the size of any other in view, the bulk of a large house. The side that loomed over him as he confronted it was nearly flat. Had some natural force cloven the stone, long ago, or some magic? Certainly magic had been at work here, for a symbol had been chiseled into this face. Its boundary was a circle, a fathom across. Otherwise it was so eroded that he could only see it was of labyrinthine complexity..

Did it, though, bear kinship to signs he had encountered on cliffs in the South? Brandek bent close in wonderment. His forefinger tried to trace faint lines and curves. A shiver went through him as he identified a *vai*, that letter of the hieratic alphabet which was never used in writing. The memory of how potent it had been in gramarie was still too sharp.

The raven flapped overhead. Somehow, abruptly, that winged blackness reminded Brandek of Llangru and the boy's claims about faring forth in animal guise. It didn't seem like childish fabulation. Llangru was too desperately serious about it. He didn't even act like a child trying to deny that his father was dead, trying in a way to *be* that father and wield forces which themselves were forever vanished.

But if he wasn't daydreaming or play-acting, what then? Brandek's lips tightened. He had seen more than one person driven by despair to seek refuge in delusion. And those had been able-bodied adults. Llangru, frail and unripe soul in a body that from birth had been encumbered—Was Llangru simply insane?

Poor Shalindra. . . . Impulse outraced thought. Brandek retraced the sign while he spoke its name, "*Vai*," which means "I guard."

Earth rumbled and grated. Through his bootsoles and into his bones, he felt shock waves hit. The great stone shuddered. Lesser boulders toppled or rolled. In a tidal roar, the scree poured downward.

Brandek spun on his heel and bounded ahead of the slide. If those shards caught him, they would cut him into flitches. It flashed across his mind—a wisp of power to hold mountains in place had remained in yonder emblem. He drained it off when he uttered the formula. Ripsnarl slumped further.

A hammerblow cast him into night.

As he returned to day, he was not aware of pain. Instead, he was dazedly surprised by the silence. So vast was it, after the noise before, that he lay in it as if in ocean depths, as if he had become a merman. The wind around the peak sounded fugitively faint. His heartbeat was no louder.

He tried to raise himself. Then the agony smote. Darkness blew ragged across his vision. He heard his voice scream.

After a while he grew capable of careful small

movements, and thus of learning what had happened to him. His right shin lay across a track plowed by the round rock which had overtaken him and come to rest several yards off. Though his mind was still clumsy and anguish dragged at every thought, he decided that it had knocked him down and passed over his leg. Soil had cushioned him somewhat, little blood seemed to have been lost, but he saw the slight bend under his knee. That, as well as what he felt, told him the shinbone was broken.

His right arm wouldn't obey him, either. Every attempt at motion sent lightnings through him. The upper bone was likewise fractured. He guessed he had fallen with arms flung out and landed on that one in just the wrong way, the force of the boulder behind him.

The rest of his body throbbed within his garments, he must have bruises from head to foot and be missing a good bit of skin, but there didn't seem to be anything worse the matter. Not that that would make much difference. He had barely escaped the talus. Pieces lay around him, and the main mass now began mere feet away. Higher aloft, half buried, the runic stone looked strangely forlorn.

Brandek almost wished the slide had caught him. He'd be free of this torture—No!

He began to curse. He cursed the mountain up the west side and down the east, roots and crown and the stupid god who erected it, for minutes, with the riches of oath and obscenity that a sailor commanded. It cleared his head and brought back a measure of strength. When he was done, he was ready to fight.

To remain here was sure death; Cren and Destog would never find him in time. The odds were overwhelming that they never would at all, nor any search party they might fetch. But at least if he had water he would live longer and thus have a tiny chance. Moss in the hollow that he had noticed betokened moisture. A frightful distance to go, in his present state: but the only way for him.

He rolled to his left side, overbalanced, and fell prone on grit and flinders. Pain seethed; icy sweat spurted forth, runneled inside his clothes and reeked in his nostrils. He mastered himself. The spears and pack of rations on his back had toppled him. With his usable hand and his teeth, he loosened their thongs. The ax he must leave behind, but he would not be without food and some means of doing battle.

With one arm and one leg, dragging his gear, he crawled.

Often in the hours that followed, the pain wore him down. He must lie half conscious, shivering, until at last he could hitch himself onward. The sun descended; the horizon flamed above far Tyreen; stars blinked forth overhead; his breath smoked in deepening cold, and he saw frost form on the stones over which he crept.

When he reached his goal, it was past midnight and he knew he could travel no more. The moss was soft and dank under his belly. A rivulet trickled through it. He sucked up water for a very long time before his body stopped feeling withered and merely hurt. By now he was almost used to hurting. It should not keep him from the rest that was his next necessity. Of course, he thought in a distant part of his mind, water like this must draw animals. Maybe big flesh-eaters were among them. Somehow he got to the largest of the boulders which loomed murkily around, that he might have his back against it. He arranged his weapons ready to his left hand, and toppled into unawareness.

That night Llangru cried Brandek's name in his sleep, but when Shalindra went to comfort him he turned toward the wall. He was silent and listless all the following day. By sunset he lay feverish, making small-animal sounds. Shalindra poured him a decoction of willowbark—that potion, at least, still worked —but he gagged on the bitterness.

"Brandek . . . broken . . . freezing . . ." Again and again, the same words. Shalindra struggled with her pride, conquered it, and sent for Brandek, merely to learn that he'd gone hunting the day before yesterday. *Right after we quarreled.* When he returned—let it be soon!—she would ask him to see Llangru. He would come for the boy's sake, no matter how angry he was with her. He was gruff but kind. His gifts had fed them through the winter, and he had never sought anything in return, despite her being a woman and alone.

Her cheeks burned. Why even think of that? Brandek could have any of a dozen girls, young, sturdy helpmeets and childbearers. Doubtless he had made his choice, and would soon wed. No matter for her concern. They could not talk together without flying at each other.

After he came back she would strive to be pleasant for Llangru's sake. Against a sudden dread: of course he would come back. The sea itself had not slain him. He was a veteran hunter.

That evening Destog brought word to his father, Kiernon the smith. He and Cren had drawn lots, and the latter stayed behind to search, though they held scant hope. They'd seen no smoke, and, in yonder trackless country full of half-mythic beasts . . . .

Shalindra was on her way home from the Lord Mayor's palace. She'd sought wine for Llangru, and had been told that Tyreen's precious and dwindling store was not to be wasted on a useless witling. Beyond the door of the Green Merman she heard voices mutter, and Brandek's name was mentioned. She entered and saw Destog; were they back from the hunt already?

". . . get a large party to search for him," Destog was saying. "Surprising he'd come to grief, but, well, I had the notion his mind was mostly elsewhere."

"What will we *do?*" That was Kiernon's basso. He spread work-roughened hands.

Shalindra had to know. She drew her cloak about her and stepped full into the ill-lit room. Soapstone lamps, newly made, guttered on shelves and the table. Brandek's design. Their smoke, combined with man-sweat and stale beer, stung her eyes. The men hushed their talk. Many more than usual were present; they must have gathered to discuss appalling news. Benches scraped as some of the older ones rose. The youngsters eyed her with indifference.

"I overheard—" she said into the abrupt silence, "someone is missing? Brandek?"

"Aye, lady," Gilm slurred. He was far-gone in drink. "Destog, here, brought word. Away in the chaos country, they were, and him beyond finding in that jumble, I'm thinking."

Shalindra turned pale. Her knees buckled and she slid to the floor.

Gilm lurched forward, slopping his beer. "Catch her, quick! Eh, there, what ails ye, lady?" He rose and shook his head. "She's fainted. We'd best get her home. Funny thing, her takin' on like that, she and Brandek was never friends."

Again it was night and the stars mercilessly brilliant. Among them the Silver Torrent glimmered along a frozen course, and sometimes a meteor darted. Though the moon had not yet risen, light was enough to show hoarfrost pale on rocks and moss, and the rivulet agleam. Its tiny tinkle was the only sound Brandek could hear, save for the breath that rattled through his lungs. By dawn the water would be ice.

He drew his good knee under his chin and hugged his good arm around it, trying to hold a trifle of warmth. If he just had his sleeping bag, he could crawl into that. But it was back in camp. Cold had soon wakened him last night. During the day he had gotten some rest. Now came the long watch until morning. It might be as well this way—lions, wolves, and their ilk did most of their work after sunset—but it deepened the weariness in him, hour by hour.

He had no means of kindling fire, and the fire in his body smoldered low. Pain was lessened a little. Partly that was because he had splinted the broken leg, lashing it to a spearshaft grounded in his boot, and kept the broken arm inside his coat with the hand under his belt. However, he recognized that whatever slight relief he felt was also due to the numbness of fatigue.

How long had he to live? Water was here in plenty, and food sufficient; you didn't leave rations unguarded for animals to find, but packed them along. He had scant appetite, must indeed force himself to fuel his flesh against chill. Yes, he thought, starvation would not move in on him as fast as exposure and exhaustion.

He downright wished that a beast of prey would arrive first. He meant to go out fighting, no matter how feebly, and to thrust a spear down the gullet of a bear was better than to sit trying to defy these nights, like Shalindra defying the future.

Better? Easier? She had never borne a weapon, but she had overcome more than he could imagine, by enduring it. How far away, how dreamlike she seemed.

—He started out of a drowse. What? The sound repeated. *Hoo-oo* . . . an owl. His bad side protested as he turned his head in search.

The owl had landed on a tall rock not far off. It was one of the great white ones that were moving south ahead of the glaciers. Starlight filled its eyes and made it doubly spectral. *Hoo-oo*, it said again. In a dull fashion, he wondered why. The tone was softer than he had ever heard before from its kind, almost caressing.

Bitterness surged in him. "Oh, yes," he said aloud, "you're welcome to pick my bones, but not till I'm done with them." He fumbled about, closed fingers on a stone, and threw it left-handed. He missed, of course. Yet it should have frightened the owl off. It didn't. The bird simply cocked its head and continued to stare at the man.

A shudder which was not from cold passed through him. He had found to his woe that a ghost of magic lingered in this desolation. It was gone, but was there more?

The owl spread wings. For a moment it held quiet thus, like a talisman of snow. Then it lifted. In three silent circles, it swung over Brandek's head before departing westward.

Gilm and Kiernon bore Shalindra to the library and sent Risaya, Hente's daughter, to care for her and her ailing son. The tall young woman sat by the fire and stitched skins, her movements deft.

Garments for Brandek? Shalindra wondered, and began shaking anew, despite her warm wrap. Finally she spoke. "How—how is Llangru?"

"Much the same." Risaya said. "He was sleeping when—oh, here he comes!"

Wraithlike, the boy padded into the main room. His nightshire hung loose, and his face seemed all huge blue eyes, with the strange gray ring around the iris. He held out his palms to the hearth. "Brandek has no fire," he said. "He shivers at night."

Risaya dropped her sewing. "What did you say, boy? How can you know anything about Brandek?" Her tone was shrill. She gulped and gathered back her work.

"Surely you dreamed it," Shalindra said. "You've been feverish." But Llangru had fallen ill before word of Brandek came. He had not left the library. How could he know?

Llangru shook his head. "You always say I dream things, Mother, or scold me for making them up. But I was there. I just got back. I *know.*"

"We've all heard your wild stories," Risaya jeered. "No one believes them. You should be ashamed. What would Brandek say?"

"Brandek never laughs at me. I saw, and I *know.*" With an attempt at dignity, the boy stumbled from the room.

He scurried down dark streets to the Green Merman. Inside, men still huddled and talked. "We've got to go out tomorrow and search," Destog argued. "We can't quit until we're sure."

"Ah, he's dead already," Hente mumbled, "as will we all be soon. Probably lose half our party in the jumbled lands. It's not worth it, just to bring home a corpse."

Llangru shivered. Most of these persons thought him half-witted, and their children taunted him, but he had a duty. He stepped forward into the lamplight. The greasy beer-soaked table reached to his breast.

Laughter greeted him. "A bit young for taverns, aren't you, boy?" Terbritt japed. And from Gilm: "Is your mother all right? Do she and Risaya know you're out?"

Llangru took a deep breath. Now, more than ever, he must not stammer. "I-it's Bran-Bran-Brandek. He-he's alive. I know where he is."

Mirth barked around the table. "I, I, I do so. *I saw him.*" He gulped. "He's on the west face of Ripsnarl, near the bottom. There was an avalanche. You couldn't find him 'mongst all those rocks, but I found him from above, and on my way back I noticed how to get there on foot. I can guide you."

Laughter tried to start afresh, but sputtered into silence. They stared. A couple of them drew signs in the air. After many heartbeats, Destog rose from his bench and whispered, "How did you do that?"

"I went. I flew." Llangru struggled against tears. "He's hurt, Brandek is, his leg and his arm both. He's freezing, and I saw lions not far off, hunting, only there wasn't any game nearby, so they'll be hungry and look farther tomorrow—" The tears burst forth, but on a tide of rage. Llangru clenched his fists and stamped. "And you sit here!" he screamed. "He taught you how to hunt, and make weapons, and keep food, and, and everything . . . and the first time *he* needs help, you just sit here!"

Kiernon the smith chewed his lip and stared at the table. Hente muttered, "The boy's crazy," and Lari whispered, "Magic is gone."

Then Fyrlei said, most quietly, "It has seemed thus. But now I wonder if a little remains after all."

Llangru swayed back and forth. "Ay-ah, ay-ah," he chanted, "it's cold and dark, the man lies by the water, hurt, he cannot run, and lions prowl. I found him, he did not know me and threw a stone at me, but I came back to take you to him. Ahh—Hoo-oo, hoo-oo." His fingers crooked like talons. In the flickery gloom, his eyes seemed to glow golden.

Destog took a step forward and reached out a hand. The boy shrank back. "NO!" he coughed, in a voice not altogether human.

Most of the company sat stiff, or leaned away as

far as they could without rising and perhaps drawing that eerie gaze. Fyrlie kept moveless, save for the lips within his white beard that said, "Here is either madness indeed, or something new and powerful. If it is simply madness, what do you risk by heeding?"

A flame leaped in Destog. "Yes!" the youth shouted. "Llangru, the *men* of Tyreen will follow us."

Kiernon rose massive to his feet and said, "Count me among them when we're ready, son. That won't be till dawn, I suppose, and most won't be in shape to travel as fast as you. But we ought to reach Brandek by tomorrow's eventide, if this—" his tone stumbled—"this child really is a seer." He forced a smile. "Meantime, suppose I try persuading his mother to let him go along."

The sun went down once more. A single crimson streak marked the place, beneath the purity of a westering planet. In that direction the sky was green; eastward it darkened to violet and the earliest stars trod forth. There Ripsnarl peak stood windless under its snows. This would be another clear upland night, cold, cold.

Brandek woke when the lion roared nearby. He was barely half aware of that noise or what it meant. His skull seemed hollowed out, he could no longer sense a heartbeat, and pain was like the rocks everywhere around, eternal but apart from him.

Yet when the beast surmounted a ridge of debris and poised on top, he felt a certain comfort. Here came his last battle, and then peace. She was a lioness, her tawny flanks vague in the dusk but eyes luminous in the forward-thrusting head. He did see

her tail switch, and heard the rumble from her throat.

Brandek reached for a spear. Sitting, he braced its butt against the boulder on which he leaned. If he was lucky, he might catch her charge on the sharp-flaked point. Doubtless that would not kill her, but she'd know she'd been in a fight.

A second and a third lioness appeared on either side of the first. A new roar echoed among the stones; their male waited behind them. Brandek sighed. "Very well," he said. "This'll be quick, anyhow."

Something stirred at the edge of vision. He glanced aloft and saw an arctic owl. Was it the same as last night's? It acted as strangely, wheeling about and winging off at an unnatural speed.

The first lioness finished studying him and flowed down the rubbleheap. Her comrades followed. When they reached the moss, they moved to right and left. Brandek grinned. "Don't worry," he croaked. "I'm not about to make a break for it."

The lead lioness gathered herself for the final dash.

"Yaaah!" cried from above. Brandek saw a hand ax—his own design—fly through the air, end over end. It struck her in the ribs. That was a heavy piece of flint, with keen edges. He heard the thunk. Blood ran forth, black in this dimness. She growled and crouched back. Her companions went stiff.

Brandek twisted his head around and saw men spring from between the boulders, into the hollow. They brandished spears, axes, knives, torches, they threw stones, they formed a wall in front of him. More by voice than sight, he recognized Cren, Destog, Kiernon, Wisnar—He fell into an abyss.

—When he came to himself, he was lying among them. They squatted, stood, danced, babbled their joy or bellowed their triumph. Few more stars were in sight; he had not been unconscious for long. The lions must be gone. Of course they would be, he thought. Animals are too sensible for bravado. They're off after easier game, to nourish themselves and their young.

Brandek's head was on Destog's lap. The youth stroked his hair with anxious gentleness. "Are you well, sir?" he breathed.

If Brandek had had the strength, his laughter would have made the mountain ring. He did achieve a chuckle. "I haven't caught the sniffles," he replied in a whisper. Wonder smote. "How did you find me . . . and this many of you?"

Awe possessed the dimly seen face above him. "Llangru."

As if that had been a signal, the boy came into sight. Men stepped aside to make a way for him. "He guided us." Kiernon's words were an undergroundish mumble. "We took turns carrying him on our shoulders, till . . . near the end, suddenly he swooned. When he woke after a while, he said we must hurry, because you were in great danger. So we did—"

The son of Shalindra knelt down at Brandek's side, smiled shyly into his eyes, and murmured, "I'm glad. You were always good to us."

Rain turned the world dull silver. It brawled over the roofs of Tyreen and gurgled between walls. The Madwoman River ran swollen, and from afar one heard the sea shout. The air was raw. Yet as she passed a hillock which had been a house, Shalindra saw that a tree which grew from it had broken into full blossom.

The door of Brandek's dwelling was never barred, for he had nothing to fear from his tribe. Besides, she came in daily to care for his needs. Nobody disputed the right of Llangru's mother to do that.

Entering, discarding her leather cloak, she must grope through weak lamplight till her pupils widened and she saw him, wrapped in furs, sitting up in bed. Restless, awkward, his left hand used a piece of charcoal to sketch plans for a weir upon a scrap of hide. "How are you?" she asked.

"Pretty well," he said. "I hobbled around some more on a pair of sticks this morning, and it didn't hurt. I can do a few things with my arm, also. Let me show you." He raised it in its splints. "Oh, yes, I'll soon be as good as new, and more annoying." His gaze sought hers. "Thanks to you," he added, not for the first time.

She winced at the memory. When he, brought back home, refused the attentions of Jayath the chirurgeon, she had gone to her books. There she found anatomical drawings. Holding those before her, she directed the sinewy hands of Kiernon as the smith properly set the broken bones. Brandek had declined wine, saying it ought to be saved for worse cases. He had not screamed. He had not even fainted. But he had lain mute and white throughout the following day.

Afterward, though—She busied herself setting forth wooden bowls and filling them with the fish she had cooked in leaves and clay and brought here in a skin. It was lucky, she thought, that in the murk he could not see how she flushed. "Everybody will rejoice to hear that," she said. "They need you."

Brandek stirred uneasily. "I hope they don't think they can't get along without me. Someday—tomorrow or fifty years hence, no matter which—they must. They've got to learn the tricks of staying alive in the world as it's become." He plucked at the wisent robe across his lap. "So much to do," he grumbled, "and I must lie in this stinking hovel. Caves, or shelters under overhanging cliffs, or tents, or . . . or nearly anything . . . would be more comfortable, and we'd get fewer people falling sick. Yes, I think Llangru would fare better too. But first we have to find our way to the *how* of such things. This very year I begin, after I'm truly on my feet again."

He sank back against a rolled-up bearskin. His left hand reached toward her. His voice dropped. "Of course," he said low, "that means the end of your books and other treasures. We can't save them if we move out. We can only take along in our heads what knowledge they give us that we can use, like how to treat fractures. I'm sorry, Shalindra."

He seldom spoke at such length, or so mildly.

She gave him his food and sat down on a bedside stool, a bowl on her knees. "It can't be helped," she sighed. "I've come to see that." As you have come to regret it, my dear, her mind added. Which is worth many books to me.

She took a chunk of fish. Utensils of metal and porcelain would presently belong to the past, like tableware. Maybe a craftsman could produce substitutes of wood, bone, or horn, but probably none would have the time. They would be too busy inventing tools more urgently needed by hunters on the fringe of the glacier. She might as well practice how to eat in mannerly wise with her fingers.

"It's the future, you know," he said. "Like it or not, it is. And you . . . you're not just borne along helpless, Shalindra. You can have a great deal to say about how it goes, in your own right and through Llangru." He paused. "After all, in spite of his power, he's still a boy. He still has much to learn from you and—and any stepfather he might get."

Her pulse, her blood cried out. She barely kept from spilling her dish.

Brandek stared at the shadows beyond his bed. "Where is he today?" he asked. "He usually comes here with you."

"He may arrive later," she replied in chosen words. "He told me he meant to—Well, do you remember Mintu, that brat who took the lead in persecuting him because he was odd? Mintu has become his most abject follower, after what happened. Llangru told me he thinks he . . . he will need helpers . . . and he had ideas about what Mintu can do. They were going to experiment with a drum and—I don't know what."

"You know more than I do," Brandek said. "I'm so ignorant about magic that I nearly got myself killed under the Heewhirlas. I'm sure of nothing except that it's not altogether gone from the world, and some of it remains in him. You, your studies—" He turned his head to her. "Can you tell me more?"

She had expected this, once he regained strength

and, with it, his liveliness of mind. Again he reached out, and this time she gave him her hand. His closed around it, hard, warm, comforting. "I've ransacked the library and my own thoughts, of course," she said, while she brought her face near his because she was talking softly. "I've discovered little. This is such a new phenomenon. However—the principle is basic, that anything different, peculiar, has a certain amount of *mana* by virtue of that same differentness. And Llangru was always a strange one, wasn't he?" Of a sudden she heard herself add, "I don't imagine any other children I bear will be like him—" and stopped in total confusion and saw Brandek's mouth curve happily upward.

The smile died. His glance went past her. She twisted about and saw Llangru.

Today the slight form moved with catlike grace. She wondered: in what shape would his soul next travel forth?—and shivered. How dank the house was. Yes, open-air life would be hard, but would in truth be healthier.

Llangru had not shed his rain-wet cape. From the cave of its hood, his gaze sought Brandek. Those eyes gleamed like a lynx's. He raised a hand in salute and declared with a gravity beyond his years, "Chieftain, Mintu's drumming sent me out of my body and I met the Reindeer Spirit. He told me a big herd of them is moving this way, and we can have plenty of meat. But he also told me this will not be—they will go elsewhere—unless we give him and them their due respect."

Breath hissed between Shalindra's teeth. Her grip on Brandek tightened.

He took the news calmly, almost matter-of-factly. "Aye," he said, nodding, "I thought it'd come to something like this."

"What do you mean?" Shalindra gasped. Llangru sat down on the floor at her feet, cross-legged, facing the brightest of the lamps.

"Why, we're no longer masters of the world," Brandek told her. "We're back *in* the world, as much as animals or trees or stones or anything. What was killing our souls was that we didn't realize this, we had no idea of where we belonged or what we should believe or how we should behave . . . . I found, myself, skill's not enough."

Understanding rushed through Shalindra. "No," she whispered, "it isn't. But we'll always have a few among us who are wise about the hidden things." She bent her mind toward her son, though her hand stayed with Brandek's. "What should we do, then, to please the reindeer?" she asked.

"I do not yet know," Llangru answered, "but I will find out."

The first of the shamans fixed his eyes upon the lamp flame.